"Smoke Gets in Your Eyes" meets **"The Rosie Project"** in this darkly funny, deeply human comedy about death, grief, family secrets, and finding love at a booming funeral camp business.

At Big Burn Funeral Services, program manager Ray Wells spends his days balancing the practical and the profound. He handles funeral pyres and farm work, comforts grieving families, and somehow keeps a rural funeral campground running on time. After years of hard living and harder regrets, Ray is learning to stay steady: to tend the flames, not throw himself into them.

Then Bonnie Betts shows up. An uninhibited, Vegas-born "Jesus girl" with more conviction than caution and an infectious laugh, she runs headlong into Right Way Ray Wells. She's come East in search of peace and family. Is she the woman who can lead him to grace? Between midnight swims and quiet prayers, Bonnie shows Ray what he's been afraid to face: that faith and desire aren't opposites but different ways of reaching for light.

THE
BIG
BURN

BOOKS ALSO BY MIKE McCORMICK

15 Years a Deplorable: A White House Memoir

Joe Biden Unauthorized

The Case to Impeach and Imprison Joe Biden

An Almost Insurmountable Evil: How Obama's Deep State Defiled the Catholic Church and Executed the Wuhan Plandemic

* * *

Mike publishes a Substack, *Midnight in the Laptop of Good and Evil* in which he reveals ObamaBiden corruption, Deep State destruction, Deep Church evil, and Deep Media malevolence. Evidence he's uncovered there has been featured in the Wendy Bell Radio Show, The Daily Mail, The New York Post, Fox News, Newsmax, One America News Network, Real America's Voice, Stephen K. Bannon's War Room, The Benny Show, and dozens of radio shows and podcasts.

Mike McCormick

THE BIG BURN

Brent Tor Books

THE BIG BURN

A Novel by Mike McCormick

Copyright © 2023, 2025 Brent Tor Books

This is a work of fiction. Names, characters, businesses, places, events, locales, and incidents are either the products of the author's imagination or used in a fictitious manner. Any resemblance to actual persons, living or dead, or actual events is purely coincidental.

https://AuthorMikeMcCormick.com/

ISBN 978-1-7337146-0-0

All rights reserved. No part of the material may be reproduced in The United States of America or in any other country by any process, electronic or otherwise, in any material form or transmitted to any other person or stored electronically in any form without the prior written permission of the author.

I dedicate this novel to my lifelong love of
reading and all the books that have made
me smile, laugh, sigh, and think. Thank
you, books!

THE BIG BURN

One

"You got to earn it, Ray."

Kim Keeney was staring straight and strong at the lanky young man who had just peeled off his T-shirt with the added booty shake of a male stripper. "And," she added, "that means you got to work for it."

Then she turned and walked off, sure-footed as a lioness in heels. "You ain't even close to that with me," she called out over her shoulder.

Ray Wells grinned at every leggy step. "Earn it, hah," he called after her.

Kim, wearing a black leather skirt and a cream silk blouse, dark hair tied back in a professional ponytail, strolled slowly to her polished black Escalade, looking exactly like what she was, a sexy young woman on her way to a business meeting. Her outfit promised power and prestige. Her vehicle promised power and prestige. Everything about her promised power and prestige, except that her business meeting was at a hospice, and she was driving a hearse to pick up a body. Kim gunned the engine and drove off without so much as a backward glance.

"Earn it, hah," Ray repeated under his breath as he dropped his sweat-dampened shirt onto a wooden bench.

"Ray, focus," said Big Tom, "pyre gets lit in three hours. Guests will be down here in two. Let's get on this."

The job was to move the body from the gravel driveway to the viewing bier. Ray nodded and pulled on his leather work gloves. About the body he knew only what he had to know — it wasn't big, it wasn't heavy, and he would soon be lighting a massive bonfire to burn it up. All the way up, like ashes to ashes, dust to dust burned up. Oh, and it was the remains of an old guy with enough money to have his family take over the campground for the weekend. Three generations. Some in tents, some in trailers, and some in motor homes. Included in the crew were some frisky granddaughters. That was good. As far as Ray was concerned, frisky females make the world go round.

The body lay on a wooden stretcher, shrouded mummy-like in white cotton sheets. Having just come from the walk-in, it was refrigerator cold, despite the rising afternoon heat.

Big Tom and Ray hefted it from the driveway to the viewing bier, gravel crunching beneath their feet. The family was due to arrive in a couple hours for final respects.

The viewing bier was a waist-high brick platform near the center of a circular gravel pad of about twenty yards in diameter. An amphitheater of grassy hillsides terraced with rows of rough wooden benches surrounded it.

After placing the body on the viewing bier, they covered it with a navy blue blanket, with Big Burn Funeral Services embroidered on it in gold. Then the two men returned to the "cooker," situated about ten yards away. The cooker was another waist-high brick structure, but being topped with an iron grate, it looked like what it was: an oversized barbecue grill for burning up dead people. Officially they referred to it as the crematorium, but unofficially it was the cooker.

Moving carefully, Big Tom Wells slid logs and kindling and paraffin accelerants under the cooker grill. His tour in Iraq had earned him, among many other awards, a Purple Heart. Unfortunately, a below-the-knee prosthetic for his left leg was part of it, too. It didn't slow him down much, for he was a deliberate man of calculated movement, but it did force him to pay close attention to his footing. Big Tom hefted a three-foot length of pine into place with a care he wished his younger cousin would someday acquire. To Big Tom, pyre setup was more than piling logs. There was a structure to it, a ceremony. A proper pyre meant a proper passage. Sanctification. If Ray had his way, every pyre would be sky-high flames and sparks. Consumption full bore.

"You be careful with her, Ray," said Big Tom. "I know she can hold her own, but that's the boss's daughter. His only daughter."

Ray passed a log to Big Tom and huffed, "Earn it, dumbest thing I ever heard."

Two

"Cold as a witch's titty," said Ray, as he directed a group of tubby, tattooed, twenty-something dudes toward a pair of coolers brimming with ice and beer.

The coolers were on the concrete floor of an open air pavilion, which had been built on a grassy knoll overlooking the cooker. The pavilion was the centerpiece of the Big Burn's Family Funeral Weekend. Rustic and durable, it housed group meals, memorial services, and, with its wet bar, the unpredictable after-parties.

Ray glanced down toward the cooker. It had been a good burn. The body had been fully and quickly consumed. The grate was glowing as red as an iron in a smith's forge. And with the flames receding, the widow, sons, daughters, and grandkids were trudging up to the pavilion. That left only the dead man's brothers and boyhood friends down at the fire, watching in thoughtful silence as his remains were rendered into ash on the glowing coals.

The cousin posse grunted in unison. Hands dove into the ice. Cans were popped open. Sport coats were removed. Ties loosened. Behind them a trio of boyfriend-less, young women eyed the oaken wine casks beside Ray. "Chardonnay or Cabernet," he said, offering a tray of clear plastic tumblers.

"Plastic cups for wine," sniffed the pudgy one in the high top Converse sneakers and an artsy smock.

"Plastic tumblers are all we got," said Ray. "No glass, guns, or phones at the after-party."

"So stupid we can't have our phones," said the tall one who was dressed sensibly like the bank manager she was.

"No, it's family time," said Ray, as he gave her a direct look, "It's what your grandmother wanted for your grandfather and the family. Phones don't work out here anyway."

"No glass," she challenged.

"Safety," shrugged Ray. "Those rules save a lot of hospital trips, especially the no guns."

"I got my gun locked up in my car," yelled a cousin posse member who was now wearing his necktie as a headband.

"Definitely the right place for it," agreed Ray, as he watched Headband Dude grab a beer in each hand.

"Hey, this Chardonnay is pretty good," said High Tops with a lift of her tumbler.

"It is good," agreed Ray. "We get it exclusively from the winery down the road."

"Damn, Amber," croaked Headband Dude, the tallest of the cousins, as he crowded up to the bank manager. "Don't you see how awesome this is? Grandfather skipped the stupid graveyard, the stupid metal coffin, and all that stupid funeral home stuff, and spent the money on a party. How awesome is that?"

"Dude, not just the party," yelled Tubby Twin Number One.

"The whole weekend," added Tubby Twin Number Two.

"Chug for Grandfather," yelled Headband Dude.

"Chug for Grandfather," yelled the others.

Sensible Amber and Little Miss Converse shrugged and hoisted their tumblers of Chardonnay. While the third, an athletic blonde in a black dress and stylish leather sandals, grabbed a Cabernet. "To Grandfather," they cheered.

Ray grinned, poured another tray of wine tumblers, and turned up the music. That brought the widow over. She looked askance at Headband Dude now spraying geysers of beer at the Tubby Twins, but then Amber thrust a tumbler of Chardonnay at her, and she downed it in a blink.

"Grandma, Grandma, Grandma," cheered the grandkids.

Then, of course, the parents came over and the grandkids scattered. Ray set out tray after tray of Chardonnay and kept the beer coolers filled. After a couple hours, half the family was blotto and the other half was caretaking them. The Cabernet granddaughter was back for her third. Of all the family, she was the only red wine drinker.

"My cousins are buttheads," she said. "I love them, but they're butt-heads."

Ray nodded as he watched Head Band Dude and the Tubby Twins play air guitars to a Santana song. "They're fine," he said. "Ain't no formula for grief."

"This is weird for me," she said. "I was hoping it would be a little more heartfelt."

"I thought it was a nice send off," said Ray. "People said nice things about your grandfather."

"But now look," she replied. "It's not really for him anymore."

Ray scanned the group. A cluster of ladies had gathered around the widow, who was dabbing her eyes. A few of the dead man's brothers and boyhood friends were across the pavilion, picking at the catering. The rest of the granddaughter crew was vaping by the dying fire. A smattering of couples had wandered back to their campsites. "I have an idea. Come with me. You can do a little gesture."

"What kind of gesture?"

"A heartfelt gesture, Indian tradition."

"Oh."

"What's your name?"

"Laney."

"Laney, I like that name," Ray said as he escorted the young woman out of the pavilion and across the grass to the tree line beyond the hilltop.

"You look like a swimmer," he said.

"Backstroke," she said. "I'm on my college team."

"No, you ain't."

Laney looked at Ray, "Yes, I am," she said.

"No, you ain't. What school?" Now Ray was looking at her, catching her eye, and she knew it.

"Penn State," she said.

"Whoa, Penn State swimming. That's awesome."

"It is good," she agreed. "Pays for school."

"Double awesome," said Ray. He stopped at a juniper tree and broke off a couple of branches, rubbed them between his palms, handed them to Laney, and then inhaled deeply from his hands. "I love a good smell," he purred as he looked into Laney's eyes. She pretended not to hear him but held his gaze.

Laney set the juniper branches on her grandfather's coals as the other granddaughters, the boy cousins, and Ray looked on. The fragrant smoke drifted upward. For a long time they watched the coals. Eventually it was just Laney and Ray. "Thank you," she said, laying her hand on his shoulder. "Now what?"

Three

Kim Keeney was up early, raking the swim beach clean for the next arrivals when Laney appeared at the far end of the swim lake. She was a bit disheveled and walking gingerly, as though barefoot. Kim shook her head with an mmm, mmm, mmm.

Ray's tidy little yurt was back there, just out of sight, in a hardwood grove. The girl was literally stumbling back to her motor home after spending the night with him.

Laney made her way to the swim dock Ray had built for himself. Kim watched as she hunted around for her sandals, slipped them on, then sauntered toward the swim beach. She was on a well-worn trail that would take her past Kim and eventually to the campground. Kim went back to her raking. Ray had taken over that far end of the lake, and she was determined to stay the hell away from anything that went on there.

The two women nodded to each other as Laney approached. Kim saw Laney had gathered up some wildflowers and a sprig of juniper. Kim called out in her most corporate tone, "Hey, good morning."

"Good morning," Laney chirped back.

"How was the ceremony?"

Laney paused for a moment, took a whiff of her flower bouquet, and said, "Nothing like I expected, but really, really good." And with a serene nod and a grin of accomplishment, she continued on toward the campground.

"Another satisfied customer," Kim muttered to herself.

Four

"Skinny dipping, that's what you did with her?" asked Big Tom as he poured a shovelful of ash onto a rectangular sifting screen. The sifter was positioned across the opening of a small aluminum garbage can.

"Well, yeah," Ray replied as he shook the sifting screen. "I always start with skinny dipping if I can. You know, the wetter, the better."

"Roger that," said Big Tom, pushing his shovel under the ash pile with a loud scrape. He loved his wood-handled square point for ash sifting. Big Tom was a traditionalist, always wood for a shovel handle — never composites.

Sifting the ash pile was Big Tom and Ray's first order of business after a burn. And with the amount of wood required to cremate a body, there was enough ash left behind to fill a ten gallon metal garbage can nearly to the brim. But it was the topmost layer, down to a depth of about four inches, that held the majority of the dead person's ash, so it was Big Tom and Ray's job to carefully shovel that layer off and place it in a clear plastic bag for return to the family.

After that was done, the entire ash pile was sifted into the garbage can. That was necessary because there were still bits of bone, teeth, and other organic matter not fully consumed. The sifting process separated that out from the wood ash. Tom referred to the organic bits found in the sifter as the "rough stuff," and he set it aside in another clear plastic bag. Later, he would pulverize the "rough stuff" in a crushing machine and add that grainy material into the plastic bag containing the top layer of ash. That bag, which at that point contained nearly all of the dead person's cremated remains, was then deposited in the large ornamental wood box.

But with modern medicine there was more to the sift than finding teeth and bone bits. Dental work, pacemakers, metal surgical items such as replacement knees all made their way into the ash pile. Gold-filled teeth, precious metal dental work, pacemakers, or other hardware were recovered in the sifter and handed over to the family in another clear plastic bag.

As the Big Burn Funeral Services site manager, it was Big Tom's duty to ensure the box containing the cremation ashes and the hardware bag were properly returned to the family. What they did with the ashes was their decision. Some families emptied the box and scattered the ashes in sentimental places. Some displayed the ashes in a place of honor. Some stored them in a closet.

The remaining sifted material, almost entirely wood ash, was not returned to the family. Distributing it was one of Ray's many duties, and he was both discrete and creative as to where he did that. Being that they were on a Christmas tree farm, there were many options.

Big Burn Funeral Services, which was the actual name of the company that conducted the Family Funeral Weekends, was a side venture of a much larger entity, the Keeney Family Farm, which ran for over two hundred acres in the green, rolling hills of Madison County, Virginia. A Keeney had farmed that land since before the Civil War.

Ken Keeney, the owner, had grown up on the farm, just as his father had, and his grandfather, and his grandfather's grandfather had. It was Ken's grandfather who first planted Christmas trees on the property in the Forties.

Ken was a widower, living on the farm with his daughter Kim, whom he treated like royalty. Motherless since just before her ninth birthday, Kim had grown up attending boarding schools. Confident and attractive, she was close to her dad, but more like a friend and business partner than a doting daughter.

It had been Ken's idea to convert part of the farm to a campground for family funerals. He had read a magazine article about Viking funerals and, WHAM, there was the idea: American families needed a place to burn their dead and comfort themselves afterwards with a big, blowout party.

Well, at least some did.

There was no arguing it was a raging success, especially with Kim's marketing wiles fueling the frenzy. After three years in business, funeral services revenue was outpacing Christmas tree revenue ten to one. All through word of mouth and Kim's outreach to hospices and hospitals.

Big Tom had started working for Ken on his farm when he had only Christmas trees — that had been after he got his medical discharge from the Army. Big Tom loved working outdoors. He had always loved Christmas as a kid, and growing the trees for family Christmases made him feel like the giver he really was. Plus, the woodsy tranquility was soothing for Big Tom, who still struggled with memories from Iraq.

But when Ken had come to him with his vision for hosting outdoor funeral pyres, complete with after-parties fit for a Viking chief, Big Tom realized they were about to start a wild ride.

And even though Ken was as crazy as a linebacker, Big Tom respected his entrepreneurial instincts. He liked Kim, too. Other than being ridiculously spoiled, she was A-Okay. That girl could sell ice to an Eskimo was one of his favorite sayings about her. So the Big Burn ride had been rewarding, at least so far.

The wildcard, though, as Big Tom was discovering, was his cousin Ray. Great helper, smart kid, but he was a boner in a baseball hat. That boy was on a collision course for a slap-and-tickle with every girl he met, including, as Big Tom was realizing, Kim.

"So, then," Ray continued nonchalantly, "you know, we're all naked and frisky, out there swimming around, and I told her about the Pleasure Palace."

"Oh, yeah, what did she say?"

"She loved it. Girls love that dirty talk."

"Yeah, I guess."

"By the way, it always amazes me how none of these girls have ever skinny dipped before. I mean, this girl Laney was a swimmer, and she'd never done that."

"Skinny dipping is an acquired taste, definitely ain't for everyone," Big Tom agreed as he poured another shovelful of ash onto the sifter.

"I mean, once she tried it, she loved it — all naked and sleek, especially when we went swimming up against each other."

"I'll bet."

"Like a couple of dolphins."

"Okay."

"Sexy freshwater dolphins is what I said to her."

"Uh-huh." Big Tom watched Ray remove little chips of bone fragments from the sifter and drop them into the "rough stuff" bag in the commemoration box.

"She liked that. And then when we got to the piggy back ride," continued Ray, "she liked that even more."

"Oh, yeah."

"Yeah, I mean, she was all wet and slidey, up on my back, and I'm running, and she's bouncing and rubbing, all grippy around my chest. And I'm squeezing her butt every step. She was giggling like a cheerleader. Then we get to my 'tipi'"— at this, Ray made the sign for air quotes with his fingers. "We start rolling around on the fur pile, and that's all it took. She was lit."

"Wait, you told her the yurt was a tipi?" Big Tom leaned on his shovel and looked inquiringly at his cousin.

"Yeah, I told her I was part Indian from my grandmother and I live in a wooden tipi," said Ray as he dropped some teeth into the "rough stuff" bag. "Told her about the fur pile, showed her my hunting bow. She got all excited. I mean, you tell a girl you're part Indian and you live in a wooden tipi, they buy it without question."

"Damn, dude, sounds like you had a good night."

"Yeah, it was. You should try it."

"Try it? What do you mean?"

"You know, you and Kelly give it a go. I'll clear out."

Big Tom shot Ray a stern glare. "Ray, Kelly and I are fine," he said.

"I think she'd like it," continued Ray. "Might even get pregnant. I know you guys are trying."

Big Tom stopped shoveling and straightened up. "Ray, I am not coming out here skinny dipping and piggy backing to get my wife in the mood. We don't need that."

"It ain't bad. It's fun. You'd like it. She'd like it."

"She probably would."

"Well?"

"No, you do the wild stuff. That's not us."

"It would be good for you guys," said Ray. "There's night magic out here."

Big Tom, shaking his head slowly, sighed at his cousin. "Ray, I am NOT piggybacking my naked wife anywhere — let alone down to your Pleasure Palace so I can DO her on your fur pile."

Ray paused. By the look on his cousin's face, he knew it was time to change the topic. "All right, all right, have it your way," he said as he wiped the dead man's ash on his jeans.

The ash removal job was complete. Big Tom fastened the top securely down on the commemoration box. "Done here," he said as he set the box on the front seat of his pickup truck. "Not much hardware to return, just a couple of teeth with gold fillings. I'll get the rough stuff pulverized, add it in, and then get it all over to the widow."

Ray nodded as he hefted the garbage can filled with the leftover ash onto the bed of the four-wheeler and bungeed it securely in place. He didn't have much time to spread it. A whole new family was due to check into the campground that morning. Ray still had to hose out the pavilion. The pace was picking up. They were doing three burns a week now. This crazy job of his was getting downright hectic.

Five

"Big Funeral is after us," Ken announced.

"Big Funeral?" Kim looked skeptically up from the salad she was preparing for herself.

Ken, Kim, and Big Tom had gathered in Ken's bright, sunny farmhouse kitchen for their regular Thursday lunch meeting. This was their chance to get everyone on the same Big Burn page. Ray was due any minute. Kim had sent him out to the garden to pick lettuce and tomatoes for her salad and the BLTs Tom was preparing.

"Big Funeral," Ken said wearily. "Well, the Commonwealth of Virginia version, at least. Man, you start something good, and the bureaucrats come after you with everything they got."

"No, kidding," intoned Big Tom, who was frying up a mess of fresh cut bacon in a cast iron skillet. "What is it this time?"

"Health department inspector," said Ken. He was seated at the kitchen table reading a letter.

"Again!" huffed Kim.

And just at that moment, Ray came bursting through the screen door with a wide wooden bowl of fresh lettuce and ripe, red tomatoes. He immediately fixed his eyes on Kim and said, "Again! That's what I like to hear!"

Kim gave Ray an icy look. "Really, Ray?" she continued.

Then he set down the bowl, palmed two humongous tomatoes, held them up at eye level, and with a broad grin aimed right at Kim, made a gentle squeezing motion and said, "Nothing better than nice juicy tomatoes."

Kim shook her head wearily and said, "Ray, I just need something big enough to slice."

"Come on, Ray," added Big Tom, "These BLTs are waiting. Wash that up."

Snickering, Ray complied, first washing the lettuce, then the tomatoes. He handed the reddest one to Kim. She accepted it with a murmured thank you and quickly and expertly diced it into her salad. "Daddy, every single one of those death certificates is one hundred percent correct. And they know it."
"Big Funeral has got to stop us somehow," said Ken. "We are a serious threat. We planted our flag right in the middle of their overpriced funeral BS, and they are terrified."

"Growing like crazy," Big Tom agreed. "Families love us. They all say so."

Kim shot a sideways glance at Ray who was washing his hands at the kitchen sink.

"And the funeral home guys don't like that at all," said Ken. "Our wait list has grown to over two weeks. I'm buying another walk-in for the extra bodies. Which is apparently what this health inspector wants to see. Hey, speaking of that, how do we do our body storage?"

Big Tom almost dropped the plate of BLT halfers he was bringing to the table. He then followed that with an awkward pause. "What do you mean?" he asked, seating himself.

"How do we do our body storage?" Ken repeated firmly. "I mean, now that we're storing bodies longer, how do we keep track of which is which?" As Kim focused in on her salad, Ken looked at Big Tom. "Well?"

"Um, well, Kim puts the toe tag on the body bag at pickup. We go by those until ceremony day, when Kelly comes in and does the final body wrap."

"So, every body bag in the cooler has a toe tag? Four body bags, four toe tags?"

"Yep, right up until ceremony prep," answered Big Tom.

"So, from arrival to burn, the only ones who see the body is us?" Ken asked. "Because when the family finally sees them, they're just laid out on the viewing bier shrouded and blanketed. Then we take the blanket off, and they see the shrouded body, but nobody knows who's under the shroud. So, there's no way we burn the wrong body, I guess is what I'm asking."

Ken, having helped himself to a BLT halfer and a handful of potato chips, was now studying Big Tom and Ray who were fixing up their plates. Kim was nibbling her salad, quiet as a bunny.

"No, there's no way we burn the wrong body," said Big Tom. "Never have, never will." And he filled his mouth with a gigantic bite of sandwich.

"Good," said Ken.

"And even if we did, it's not like anybody would know," added Ray. "I mean, it's just one family gets another family's ashes and bone bits. It's not like switching a baby at a hospital and raising the wrong kid."

Ken, Big Tom, and Kim all looked at Ray.

"Ray, are you saying we burned up the wrong body?" Ken asked drily.

"No," said Ray, his face reddening. "I'm just saying it ain't like we ever did it, but it wouldn't be that bad even if we did."

"Well, it would be awful for the family if they found out," said Kim.

"Sure would," echoed Big Tom.

"Let's not get ourselves into that mess," agreed Ken, with a look at Ray, who was now munching his BLT halfer. "Because we never have, have we, Ray?"

Ray, mouth full, shook his head emphatically.

"No, we never have," repeated Big Tom.

"By the way, Ray," continued Ken, "where do you put the leftover ash from the cooker?"

Ray finished chewing and took a long thoughtful sip of his sun tea as Ken took a bite of his sandwich. "Oh, that?" Ray said finally. "Some of it I spread out around the trees. Some I spread out on the back lot hardwoods, and some I mix in with the compost."

Almost in unison everyone but Ray stopped eating.

"Wait, Ray, you mix dead people ash from the cooker in with our garden compost?" asked Kim who was now staring at a forkful of her salad she held poised in midair. Big Tom had ceased chewing and was looking alarmingly at his BLT halfer.

"Yeah," said Ray. "Well, actually it's ash from the wood fire. It's not much dead people ash in there. We sift most of that out."

"You're fertilizing the vegetable garden with dead people ash!" shouted Big Tom. "All the lettuce, all the tomatoes!" He rose to his feet and stared at his BLT, which he now held at arm's length as though it was toxic.

"And the Christmas trees," Ray answered deliberately. "But not much of it is dead people ash. Just a micro, smidgy bit. Most of it is wood ash."

"Just a smidgy bit!" Big Tom thundered. "Dude, that's how soylent green started!"

"Ray, I can't believe you do that," hissed Kim. "That's the most disgusting thing I ever heard."

"How long you been doing that, Ray?" Ken asked calmly. He didn't seem worked up in the least.

"Since I started here, about two years now," replied Ray.

"Damn, Ray, you been mixing dead people ash in with the compost for two years?" asked Big Tom. "What do you think we are, cannibals?"

"It's good for it, balances it out."

"And you didn't tell anybody?" asked Ken.

"Nope," said Ray, as he reached for another BLT halfer.

"Anybody ever seen you?" asked Ken.

"Nope."

"So, we've had this ash in the garden for two years?"

"Yep."

Ray looked over his sandwich and met the stares of his three colleagues. "I mean, it's circle of life stuff," he said. "It's good for the compost. It's good for the trees. It's not harmful. It's just fertilizer. Ain't no big deal. It's circle of life. No big deal."

"No big deal?" demanded Big Tom. "Ray, thanks to you I'm eating freaking soylent green!"

"Dead people ash in the garden — our garden, my garden — is a big deal," echoed Kim. "I can't believe you did that."

"Soylent green, nothing," huffed Ray. "These tomatoes are red and juicy and delicious. That garden is growing awesome. And the trees have never been healthier. Every one of them is full and green. Look at this tomato. It's awesome. I'm spreading fertilizer. That's all it is."

There was a pause as the trio let Ray's defiant words sink in.

"I have noticed that about the trees," agreed Ken. "The buyers were out last week, and they were so impressed I pushed them to an extra dollar a tree. That's not bad. And you think it's because of the ash you're putting out there, Ray?"

"I think so."

"Huh," Ken forked a thick slice of fresh tomato onto his plate and dropped some salt on it.

"Plants don't care where the fertilizer comes from," added Ray.

Big Tom resumed his seat. Both he and Kim made a show of sniffing their food.

"That IS a damn good tomato," agreed Ken as he chewed contentedly. "But still, Ray, mixing the cooker ash with the compost ain't exactly kosher. I mean, while it's not bad, it can be easily misunderstood."

"I'll say," agreed Kim, who resumed nibbling her salad. "We got a brand to promote, Ray. Word gets out about you spreading dead people ash all over the farm, no one will want to come out here. You can't just go and do anything you want, Ray. You got to think about the business."

Big Tom went back to chewing on his BLT as he sniffed a tomato slice.

"I mean, it's not that it doesn't pass the smell test," said Ken. "Because it does. At least for me. How about you, Tom?"

"Yeah, okay," agreed Big Tom. "I got to admit it is a damn good tomato, and the garden is doing great. And we got piles of ash, with more on the way. We got to do something with it."

"There you go," said Ray. "And I definitely ain't putting no ash in no water supply."

"Oh, hell no, don't do that," agreed Ken.

"But, Daddy, we can't just have Ray spreading that stuff willy nilly around the farm. If word gets out, people will absolutely freak out."

Ken nodded. "Yeah, that's true. Ray, you got to understand the delicacy here. For these families that leftover ash isn't just from a wood fire. It's part of their final goodbye to someone they love — mom, dad, brother, sister, grandma, grandpa. I mean, it's like remnants of their family memories are in there, their lives are in there. So, we probably don't want them finding out we're dumping it in with a pile of horse shit."

Kim and Big Tom both stopped chewing and eyed Ken, who was now looking at Ray with the deliberate stare of a gambler who had laid his cards on the table. Ray stopped chewing.

"That said, I agree with you," continued Ken. "It is fertilizer — special, yes, but fertilizer. It ain't illegal to fertilize my farm that way. And no one is going to tell me how to fertilize my damn farm if it ain't illegal. So, Ray, I appreciate the work you're doing. I'm hearing good things about you from these families. They gush about the way you handle the parties."

At that Ray beamed, Big Tom nodded, and Kim squirmed in her seat.

"But when you fertilize, just be discreet about it. We don't need anybody getting upset and misunderstanding what we're doing."

"Yes, sir," said Ray, obviously relieved.

"Especially when you're dumping micro bits of their people in with the compost."

"Yes, sir," Ray repeated gratefully. "Discreet. Got it."

"You know, Daddy," added Kim with a girlish lilt, "what about making a memorial garden kind of thing."

"What do you mean?"

"Well," she continued, "you know how you and I visit Mommy's grave sometimes."

"Yeah," said Ken. "Up on the hill where Mommy is." And he gazed wistfully out the window, as everyone at the kitchen table grew quiet and still. "That's where I'll be going when it's my time."

"I know, Daddy, you always say that."

"I'll be up there with Mommy."

"I know, Daddy. I know you will. I know you miss her."

No one stirred as Ken stared out the sunny kitchen window that he had shared with his wife and daughter for those few best years of his life. Eventually after a minute or so, his voice husky, he asked, "What's this about a memorial garden?"

"Well, how about if we set up a memorial garden, so if anyone wants to come back out, they can go there."

"You mean like a contemplation garden?" asked Big Tom.

"Yes, exactly," said Kim.

"They come back out for a visit?" asked Ray, somewhat bewildered. "You're saying we got to build a garden place for people just to sit there and think about stuff?"

"Yes, Ray," huffed Kim. "People do that. Some people do that."

"No way."

"Because they have memories, Ray," said Kim. "Memories and feelings they need to process."

"Feelings to process," repeated Ray with a head shake, though he noticed Ken and Big Tom were nodding in agreement. Kim noticed, too. "And if we fertilize it with some of the wood ash from the cooker," she continued, "we can tell people that's what we do with it, and then it becomes their memorial garden, part of the life and growth of the farm. Like that person never really died, like they're still here, part of the plants and flowers, part of the beauty. Like Ray said, circle of life."

The three men stared at Kim, each understanding the depth of her feeling in their own different way, but to a man also knowing she was right.

"Good," said Ken. "Good idea, memorial garden. Like with some flowers and shrubs, maybe a couple little benches."

"Or picnic tables," added Ray.

Once again the trio turned their speechless attention to Ray. After a pause Ken said, "I'm not seeing it as a picnic grove, Ray — it's not like we want folks showing up with a bucket of chicken. More like a little sit-down place. But nice. Flowers and shrubs kind of thing."

"And that's where we put the leftover ash?" asked Ray.

"Well, part of it," said Ken. "You keep spreading it here and there — discreetly, mind you. But then some of it goes in the memorial garden. That way if anyone ever asks, we can tell them that's what we do with it."

"But only if they ask about it," emphasized Big Tom.

"Only if they ask," agreed Kim.

"And we're going to build a little garden for family members to come back out and comfort themselves?" asked Ray, stroking his chin. "But no picnic tables."

Kim, knowing Ray as she did, could already see the wheels spinning behind his words.

"No picnic tables," said Big Tom as he gathered up the empty lunch plates.

"I think this is a great idea, Kimmy," agreed Ken. "You and Ray make it happen."

"Me and Ray?" Kim recoiled with obvious discomfort.

"Yes, you and Ray. I've got something else going, and I need Tom to help me with that," said Ken, who exchanged a knowing nod with Big Tom.

"Make it happen," sang Ray with a little shoulder roll. "Make it happen."

"Daddy, wait, really?" pleaded Kim.

"Really," said Ken. "You have a great idea, now go make it happen. Ray, you help her."

"Make it happen, make it happen," Ray was on his feet, swaying his hips. "Memorial garden, me and Kim going to make it happen," he said with a grin.

"Now there's a guy who loves his work," chuckled Ken.

Six

"This is my first time up here," said Ray. "Been working this farm two years, know every inch, except here."

"Yeah," said Kim distractedly. She was staring at her mother's grave. Karen Cady Keeney was inscribed on the headstone. "It's our private place, Daddy and me. My grandparents are over there. All the Keeneys are — I think there were a couple of Daddy's uncles who died in World War Two and were buried in France, but other than that, they're mostly all here."

"I keep offering to come out and do the weed whacking, but your Dad always says he'll do it."

"Yeah, he comes out and talks to Mommy when he does it," said Kim.

She stood quietly for a few moments, recalling the jarring childhood memory of her father, weeping on his knees beside her mother's freshly dug grave, jamming his hands into the mound of reddish brown soil he had dug with a borrowed backhoe, clutching so desperately at dirt.

Her mother had started coughing one day and just couldn't stop. The doctors at the hospital had no answers. The ventilator didn't help. And then she was gone. Dead. It happened so fast they didn't have time to understand it was the end. There was never a moment where they thought it was the end. And then it was the end, an awful end, with a mound of dirt and a headstone where her Mother was.

Forever.

It was a swift tumble of memories Kim had kept at arm's length for many years. She could have shared them with the man standing beside her, but instead, she turned away from the gravesite. Ray turned with her, caught sight of a red-tailed hawk soaring a thermal, and lifted his eyes skyward. For a few moments he followed its effortless float as Kim surveyed her family's farm and stifled her painful memories.

They were standing on a grassy hillside, capped with a solitary white oak. The tree was just outside of a low picket fence that bordered the Keeney Family cemetery. It was a sunny July morning. The dew was still on the grass. A large field of head-high, white pine saplings spread out before them.

The vantage was a sweeping view of the farmhouse and outbuildings, most of which were now related to funeral services. There was a shiny gray metal building that had gone up only two years ago. It was the body storage and ceremony prep site. They called it the Metal Barn. With the second walk-in refrigerator having just been added, it was almost wall-to-wall with bodies waiting for their final goodbyes.

"Daddy thinks we should put the memorial garden down by the campground road," Kim said, breaking the silence. "That way people will see it when they're coming and going, and they'll know where it is if they want to come back."

"That's a good idea," agreed Ray. "We can just work it in with the trees. We should just walk around down there, and you can tell me where to put stuff, though we'll want to wait till fall for any real planting. This summer heat will scorch the hell out of anything we put out there now."

Kim nodded. "Big Tom was sure happy with his raise," she said congenially. "What are you going to do with yours?"

"Oh, yeah," sputtered Ray, surprised at Kim's overture. "Ken did right by us. Big Tom sure can use it now that Kelly is pregnant. Me, I'm going down to Virginia Beach for some deep sea fishing."

"Oh, interesting," said Kim.

"I try for marlin or tuna. I'd love to catch a trophy tuna. They can go 600 pounds and up."

"Six hundred pounds of tuna — what would you do with that?"

"Bring it back and eat it. I can store it in the walk-in with the dead people, or maybe I'll just throw it on the cooker for a fish fry," cracked Ray.

And for the next ten minutes he grinned his way through Kim's lecture on why that was the dumbest thing he could possibly do.

Seven

Sunrise, and the yurt was aglow with diffused light. Ray was awake but feigning sleep, so was the woman lying beside him.

The night shadows were vanishing with the rising dawn, and the objects of Ray's simple living quarters were once again defining themselves into existence — the wood stove in the center of the small, domed structure, with its metal chimney rising through the roof. The small table, chairs, hot plate, and mini fridge in his "kitchen." His "man cave corner," with his hunting and fishing gear at the ready. His clothes, lumped on the floor — near the condom wrapper reminder of their previous night's … activities.

And then, of course, there was her white linen dress, piled at the foot of his bed beside the sandals she had so eagerly kicked off.

They were together without touching — sharing, for the time being, his bed. She was dark-skinned with black hair, thick and silky. Risha's family had cremated her grandmother according to their Indian traditions. It was a one-day ceremony. Big campout parties were not the Buddhist way. But fire, flowers, and remembrance were.

She was older than Ray by several years, childless, married to her thriving mortgage services business. But then her grandmother had died, and she was the one who contacted Kim and negotiated a special one-day rate. She was the one who had come out alone to Big

Burn, ahead of her family to nail down the details. She was the one her brothers had bickered with as she insisted they pay their share. She was the one.

It had been a swirl of emotions, of life, of loss, of regret, of family pride and tensions. And in the midst of it all was the charming young man with the beautiful eyes. He treated her with warmth and listened to her and offered his curiously seductive observation, "sometimes you just got to flush out your pipes with a good fuck."

And so she said yes. Yes to his tent house. Yes to his blue eyes. Yes to his milky body. Yes to his dick. Yes.

But they had done it her way. Not his. Hers.

Now the morning after, it was his.

Ray reached out and rested, ever so lightly, his calloused white hand on her soft brown shoulder. Gently, almost finger by finger, he squeezed her shoulder. She did not stir. Lifting his hand till only his fingertips were touching her flesh, softly, softly back and forth he caressed her shoulder. She was still, not so much as a tremble.

He was in no hurry. Slowly, deliberately, gently using only his fingertips he caressed her shoulder and neck in long, slow strokes as if painting her outline. She was the nude. He was the artist. Her body was his canvas, his fingertips the brush.

She remained still as an artist's model. Stroke after stroke, shoulder to neck he caressed with his fingertips, yet she did not react. Steady, slow — whole hand, fingers, thumb, palm. Sweeping, stroking, petting. Not so much as a shudder.

His fingertips brushed up into her scalp, slowly ascending the fine, delicate hairs that ran up her neck, then into her hair, spreading his fingers, combing, combing, combing, running her silky hair gently through his fingers. Running her gently through his fingers.

Then to her ears, deftly rimming her lobes, fingering, touching her cheeks, her neck. Only when he caressed the base of her throat and chin with the back of his fingers, did she moan. Softly, far back in her throat, like a purr. And then she rolled to him, meeting his gaze as she lay on her back.

That was the moment of her desire. Silently, he lifted the sheet away from her and continued stroking, now down the sides of her neck. Fingertips lightly brushing over her skin. Eyes wondering at her beauty. From her neck, to her collar bones, to her shoulders, to the gentle rise of her breasts and the dark smudges of her nipples, stroking, swirling, caressing her flesh with his fingertips.

Time stopped. For both. The world outside was forgotten. Death was forgotten. Time was forgotten. There was only desire.

Ray loved women's bodies. He loved how they looked. He loved how they smelled. He loved how they tasted. He loved how they felt. He loved their sounds. He loved all of them, indiscriminately. He was the artist, they were his canvas.

Most of all, he loved their yes.

From her breasts, he swept to her belly, soft, rounded, feminine, then to her hips, and then, of course, across to the top of her fur. At that, her moaning stopped. For a long time he caressed the wiry hair guarding her area. Palm on her flesh, fingers petting the fringe. All the while she lay there, not moaning, not encouraging, suspended between yes and no.

Ray sensed her hesitance, understood she was not ready. Not yet. He moved to her feet and petted delicately at her toes, relishing her stylish pedicure, admiring, delighting in her glossy red toenails and pretty brown feet. Kneeling now, like a massage partner, he stroked her ankles, her Achilles' tendon, the whole of her smooth shaven legs — shins, calf muscles. She moaned again, ever so slightly, when he massaged the sensitive skin at the back of her knees. Then to the top of her thighs, caressing. Now she was watching, hands behind her head, observing him, observing herself, observing their desire, and that was when she moved for him, spreading her legs, opening herself for all of him to be with all of her.

Yes.

Eight

"Kelly's happy as could be," said Big Tom. "Starting to show. Eating like crazy. Boobs are getting bigger."

"Really?" asked Ray. "Like with the milk?"

"Well, not exactly with the milk yet, but she's getting there. Got our Little Peanut growing inside her."

"Dang," said Ray. "I am so happy for you guys. You and Kelly are going to be great parents."

Ray and Big Tom were in the back of the Wood Barn, one of the farm's original buildings. They were seated on five-gallon plastic paint buckets. They were lashing up the stretchers the pallbearers used to place the body on the cooker. It was a job they did every couple of weeks so they always had plenty of stretchers on hand, which was even more important now that the business was taking off.

The stretchers were all the same design — ladders, basically, made of untreated 2x2s in which the rungs were lashed to the rails with binding twine. Some of the rungs extended out into pallbearer handles — three on each side. That way, once all commemorative speeches were concluded, six family members could easily heft the stretcher from the viewing bier to the cooker, at which point Ray would light the pyre.

And while the lashed-up stretchers looked primitive, the design promoted a quick, all-consuming burn. Plus, there were no nails or screws that had to be dug out of the ash afterward. That design had been Big Tom's idea. Ken had praised him mightily for it.

"How was that ceremony with the Indian folks?" asked Big Tom. "Did you give them their box?"

"Yeah," said Ray. "I took care of it. Glad you and Kelly had some time together."

"Yeah, appointment with the midwife. Thanks for covering."

"Any time," said Ray. "Yeah, they were definitely satisfied customers, especially the cougar that caught me."

"Cougar, you got caught by a cougar?"

"Man, I got scratches and everything. She was wild. Wait, they got tigers in India, right?"

"Yep, tigers in India."

"Well, then she was a tiger not a cougar. Tiger woman from India."

"Tiger woman from India, that's funny. So, did you pull the 'I live in a wooden tipi, my grandmother was an Indian BS?'"

"No, not at all. She would have seen through that in a second. She was a sharp lady."

"So, lady not girl?"

"Oh, no girl. Lady. Definitely lady, very classy — has her own business, something with real estate. Drives a Jaguar. She gave me her business card."

Big Tom laughed: "Oh, man, she's definitely regretting that, especially if you show up at her office with your cammo and work boots."

Ray joined in, laughing at the thought. "No, that ain't me," he said. "I ain't no stalker. She don't need me showing up at her office and messing up her business."

"What if she wants you to?"

"Then she'll call. But they never do. What happens at the Big Burn stays at the Big Burn. I think that's why she went all tiger woman. She came out here for her grandmother's funeral, and there I was. We hit the Pleasure Palace, and she unleashed herself."

"Oh yeah."

"I mean, she threw me down, jumped up on me like a tiger."

"Damn."

"No inhibitions. I'm talking no inhibitions. And there wasn't a whole lot of talking going on."

"Roger that," said Big Tom, as he checked his lashings with a couple of tugs.

"I mean, at one point I reach up to rub her pretty brown boobies and she grabs my hands and starts rubbing herself all over with my hands."

"Yeah?"

"Like she was in the shower and my hands were her soap, just rubbing herself all over with my hands, just so sexy."

"Uh-huh."

"And I just lay there and let my hands go limp, you know how they tell you to do when you get fingerprinted?"

"Yeah, sort of."

"That's what I did. And I'm lying there, looking up at her rubbing my white hands all over her pretty brown boobies, and I'm thinking I am the creamy white stuffing in the sexiest Oreo cookie there ever was."

Big Tom laughed: "You're crazy, dude. You crack me up."

Nine

"I want crushed white marble for the walkway," said Kim, pointing downward to the ground.

"Crushed white marble?" asked Ray. He was walking a few steps behind Kim, ogling.

"Yes, Ray, the echo person, that's what I said, crushed white marble," she said, as she, knowing what he was up to, turned to face him.

Kim and Ray were walking the string lines Ray had laid out for the memorial garden pathway. Kim was pleased with how he'd made the path wind through the trees as she had directed.

It was mid-morning. Ray was dressed for the work he'd been at since sunup — muddy boots, blue jeans, and a white cotton T-shirt. Kim, not usually an early riser, was dressed for a client-free day on the farm — chukka boots, jeans, flannel long-sleeve unbuttoned over a white camisole, and her beloved Lady Akubra hat she got from the Aussie shop.

"See, I was thinking more like campground gravel," added Ray. "Mostly because we already got a pile of it."

"No, we are not putting that plain old gravel on my garden walkway."

"Well, crushed white marble is pricey, Kim. Like super extra pricey. How about just gray gravel, like we already got laid all around the campground and cooker? We got a pile of it behind the Wood Barn. I can start spreading that today."

"Crushed white marble, Ray, is what I said because crushed white marble is what I want, and that's what we're going to have here."

"Why?"

"Because it will look beautiful, Ray. It will look classy and elegant, like a garden at a Tuscan villa. That's what I want."

Kim took note of Ray's puzzled look. "Tuscany is a region in Italy," she sighed. "I stayed at this beautiful old farmhouse there once on a high school trip. The villa and gardens went back to Roman times. Crushed white marble is what they had on their walkways. I'll never forget it. That's what I want here."

"Well, Kim, I'm sure your crushed white marble was pretty in Italy," drawled Ray. "But this is Madison County. I'm not sure it works here as well as the gravel we already got."

"Ray, we're not creating this garden for Madison County. We're creating it for our guests. People appreciate when you make an extra effort for them. And we're going to make this elegant because that's comforting and memorable. Which is why we call it the... Memory Garden. Here's the list of plants we're going to put alongside my beautiful crushed white marble walkway... that I am sure I will have."

Kim handed Ray a yellow sheet of legal pad paper on which she had in her own neat cursive handwriting listed a series of ornamental plants. Ray scanned the list and scratched his head. "These are the plants you want. Why do you want these?"

"Because I want them, Ray. And why do you have to question everything I want? Daddy put me in charge, not you. All you need to know is what I want and then you make it happen. 'Make it happen, make it happen,' wasn't that your little song?"

Ray looked sternly up from the paper. "Kim, Ken asked me to help you with this idea of yours, and I am helping you — and him — and the business. These are some pretty plants you have on this list, and I have two words for them: deer food."

At that, Kim locked eyes with Ray. "Look around, Kim," he continued. "This ain't Italy, this ain't Home and Garden Magazine, this is Keeney Family Farm. There's a herd of deer out here, and we're standing in their bedroom. And these deer poo where they sleep. See that deer poo. It's all through here. That means it will be all over your crushed white marble. Big piles of it. And all these fancy plants you want, that's their bedtime snack. They will chew through them like a lawnmower."

Kim looked around at the extensive deer sign Ray was pointing out, and then crossed her arms and turned to him and said, "Ray, you're not hearing me: Crushed white marble is what I want, and these are the plants I want. And if we have to chase the deer away, well, we'll just chase them away."

"How we going to chase them away?"

"We can drive out here and honk horns and bang pots."

Ray studied Kim, hoping for a glimmer of a smirk that revealed she was actually joking. There was none.

"Honking horns ain't going to work, Kim. Think it through. First of all, you'd have to be out here all night, like almost every night. Not only will you sound like a dipshit, you will feel like a dipshit because it ain't like it chases them away. They just move off and come back when you leave. It ain't going to work, and I ain't doing it. Big Tom ain't doing it. Ken ain't doing it. You'll be out here all alone, honking your horn all night like a dipshit, and I guarantee you will not be popular with campground folks."

Kim gave Ray a belligerent stare. "Ray, this garden is going to look the way I want it to look — not the way you want it to look, not the way the deer want it to look, but MY way. White crushed marble for the walkway, a couple of concrete benches, and some pretty plants. And I agree that we may need some deer-proof plants. But if the deer are messing up the garden, we'll have to just hunt 'em out of here."

"Hunt 'em? What do you mean hunt 'em?"

"Really? Again with the echo? Get your bow and hunt them out of here, Ray. If they're pests, get rid of them."

"Whoa, whoa, Kim, hold up. You want me to kill a deer herd for a garden? Hell, that ain't right. It ain't even a vegetable garden. It's just a sit and think garden. All you got to do is deer-proof it. There's all kinds of plants you can put out here they won't eat."

"Or we can get rid of them and do the garden my way, which is the best way."

"Kill a deer herd so you can have your way? Just cancel them right off the face of the Earth, is that it?"

"Yes, that's it. That's exactly it."

"Kim, I ain't doing it. I don't care what it costs me, but I ain't doing it. That old buck who runs that herd has a rack bigger than the grill on my truck. I ain't killing an animal like that for a garden. He ain't no pest. He's just out here doing his job — eating, shitting, and fucking. That's a buck's God-given job, and he's good at it. He ain't done nothing wrong till you decided to make him wrong by infiltrating his bedroom. Now, I might take a couple does out of here in the fall. But I ain't taking that old buck. He belongs on Keeney Family Farm as much as we do."

"You don't belong here, Ray. I do. My name is Keeney, yours is Wells. I live here. You work here. And right now you're working for me, and I'm telling you what I want."

"Well, I ain't taking that buck. Your dad will back me up on that. He loves that buck, too. He talks about him all the time. You kill that animal, you will kill the spirit of this farm. And you know it."

Kim shifted on her feet, but said nothing.

"So, yes, Kim, I am working for you… for your dad… and for that buck. And for me. I'm working for all of us. So, yes, there's still going to be droppings everywhere. And yes, if you have to have crushed white marble, I'll lay the path out with it just so you can have your Italy garden, and then, yes, I'll come out and make sure it's clean and pretty, fit for our guests. One more job I got to add to my ever growing list — sweeping deer shit off the fancy path. But that's okay, because I ain't killing that buck."

"Just get the crushed marble, Ray. Have it in by next week. Make sure it looks good. When it's time, plant whatever deer-proof plants will work."

"Yes, ma'am," huffed Ray, as Kim stalked off.

Ten

Ray gunned the chainsaw and in one smooth stroke sliced a three-foot section off the trunk of a large white pine. Soft wood, easy cut, pine sawdust showering his shirt, jeans, and boots. He walked his way alongside the tree. Ten cuts, ten sections.

While Ray was sectioning the trunk, Big Tom was working on the limbs. It was a job Big Tom liked. He truly enjoyed wrestling with the limbs and then cutting them into kindling with a lopper and a handsaw. He liked the efficiency of it. Everything but the needles and twigs would be burned for a pyre, and the needles and twigs left behind would just blend in with the forest floor. It was satisfying to start and end the job all right there, and leave nothing to waste. After what he had seen in Iraq, waste was the real enemy.

The pine grove formed the lower slope of the broad mountain that dominated the farm's western boundary. It had always been a special site for Ray. His family legend was that it used to be Wells land, lost long ago in the aftermath of the Civil War.

It was a place of quiet shadows, carpeted with a thick loam of spongy pine needles. The air was evergreen fresh. The trees, stately, tall, and stoic. Some were older than the farm. Something about their quiet made Ray want to lift his eyes and think about God. If that pine grove was the closest he'd ever get to a cathedral, that was okay by him. He'd do his God talking out there.

They had driven up the dirt road into the pine grove in Big Tom's

4x4 pickup, splitter in tow. While Big Tom busied himself with the kindling, Ray set up the splitter. After Ray finished cutting the pine logs, he set them into the splitter and pulled the lever for the kinetic arm to slam them into pieces. Once he got all his tree trunks split up, he'd throw the logs on top of the kindling Big Tom was piling in the truck bed.

They split the pine green and unseasoned because they burned it green and unseasoned. Half green pine, half seasoned hardwood was Tom's preferred ratio for the pyres. Ray liked two-to-one pine to hardwood because it burned high and hot. But Big Tom disliked the excessively smoky pine fires.

The argument about the proper ratio of pine to hardwood was a constant between the two cousins, but it was always good natured, and it always went Big Tom's way. Mostly because he was more senior, but also Ray understood that Big Tom hated big plumes of black smoke. As he'd often said, he'd seen way too damn much of that in Iraq, and it was always bad.

Once they had filled the truck bed with every scrap of wood they could fit, Ray hitched the splitter up, and they paused for a water break.

"That Little Peanut is growing like crazy," Tom declared proudly. He and Ray were side by side, leaning against the truck bed on the driver's side.

"Kelly looks great," said Ray.

"She could not be happier. Getting bigger. Eating funky stuff. Banana, bacon, and peanut butter sandwich last night."

Ray laughed. "Damn, that sounds like something I might eat."

"She liked it. I made it for her. It wasn't bad. It's amazing how something so tiny changes your life so much."

"Boy or girl?"

"Don't know and don't want to. God has blessed us. That's all we need to know."

Ray nodded and took a deep drink of melted-ice water.

"But you and I are going to get real busy, dude," said Big Tom. "This expansion Ken has got us on is big — real big. And now Kelly's pregnant, and we got a little baby coming in on top of it."

Ray chuckled, "You know, I thought Ken was giving us that raise for all the work we had done, not what he was lining up."

"That's how Ken rolls. But I got to say that second campground, on that parcel by the stream... I mean, guests will love it."

"And Ken will love the money," said Ray.

"And Ken will love the money," agreed Big Tom. "But we're getting a pretty good chunk of that. This ain't no farm job anymore, Ray. We are a growing enterprise. We get that second campground up and running, it's going to pay off big time. And you should know this, and I'm saying it because we're out here, all by ourselves, but Ken wants me to go down to Florida with him and set up Big Burn Florida."

"What?"

"For real. All the old folks down there, it will be a gold mine."

"Damn."

"Exactly. And that would leave you up here, raking it in with Ken and Kim. Play your cards right, my man."

"Me and Ken and Kim. Oh, yeah, I'll play my cards right."

"No, seriously, Ray, don't screw this up. This is a big opportunity for you. But you got to understand Kim is out of your league. You just got to get that."

"Ain't nobody out of my league."

"She sure has got something to say about it. It ain't all you. Every indication I see from her is she is out of your league."

"Dude, ain't nobody out of my league. They all come around eventually."

"Well, just watch it with Kim. She ain't a 'they,' she's an us. Don't mess this up. Ken wants to be the king of alternative funeral experiences."

"Alternative funeral experiences? Is that what we're calling it now?"

"Catchy, huh. That's what Kim came up with."

"Alternative funeral experiences... shoot."

"Not shoot. Goldmine. He's talking franchises. I mean, we could be on the ground floor of being set for life."

"Franchises, you mean like Burger Bro's?"

"Probably not as many as Burger Bro's, but, yeah, something like that."

"Damn, I mean, I can see Ken pulling it off, and I'm pouring everything I got into this job. And if there's more work, bring it on. Work first, then play. It ain't nothing with me and Kim, at least not yet."

"Okay, now you're talking. By the way, Ken's cousin's daughter from Vegas is coming East. She might be popping up around here. He got her a job with Bev and Myrna. We'll see how that goes."

"She's with Bev and Myrna? Is she gay?"

"I don't know. I don't think so. Bonnie is all I know."

"Bonnie from Vegas."

"Yeah. All Ken said was she was his cousin's daughter. The cousin he went out and visited every year. She died a few years ago, and he's kind of looking out for her daughter."

"Where's the dad?"

"Doesn't sound like there is one."

"Oh. So Ken is stepping in?"

"Yeah, helping her out."

"He's good like that."

"Yeah, he is," agreed Big Tom.

"Well, if she's from Vegas she'll fit right in with Bev and Myrna, even if she ain't gay."

"We'll see. All I know is Ken got her in with Bev and Myrna because as busy as we're getting with all this expansion, they're cooking and cooking and cooking. I mean, they're catering their nice, little old lady lesbian behinds off."

"Yeah, they are," laughed Ray. "We are all getting extra busy. Bonnie, huh? Okay, I'll keep an eye out for her."

"But, Ray," added Big Tom, as he opened the driver's side door of his truck. "I'm telling you, don't screw this up. Don't go and be Wrong Way Ray."

"Stop worrying," said Ray as he moved past Tom and walked around the front of the truck. "I ain't going to mess this up. I'm done with all that. There ain't no Wrong Way Ray no more."

Eleven

Ray's eyes blinked open to the sound of snoring — loud, raspy snoring. The kind of snoring that comes after a night of heavy drinking.

It was, indeed, morning-after snoring. Ray looked over the sleeping form of the young woman lying beside him on the dock and recalled her boozy antics.

He was not smiling at the recollection.

They were sleeping rough, out under the stars on the swim dock. He had brought out the foam mat and furs off his bed. He hadn't wanted her vomit in his yurt, so they had spent the night out on the dock.

"Hi, I'm Cindy. But you can call me Sinful Cindy," was how she had introduced herself to him.

"Ray," he had offered with a hesitant nod.

That was in the pavilion after Cindy's grandfather's cremation when Ray was manning the wine bar. But she was the only family member partaking of Ray's offerings, and she was gulping them down two tumblers of Chardonnay at a time.

Before long she had returned for more, this time sing-songing, "Hi, Ray, I'm baaaaaaack."

"You sure are," he had replied in a pleasant noncommittal way.

"Join me in a drink," she had invited, sloppily.

Ray had looked around, noted the strange, subdued vibe of the gathering. They were a small group, about twenty, but certainly not what he'd describe as intimate. They had struck Ray as more like a gang than a family, kind of around each other but not really for each other. And they kept to themselves. None of them had been back to him for wine or beer, preferring the liquor from their pocket flasks. The fire was what unified them. They sat huddled around it, drawn to it as if it was a television screen. Nor was there much conversation. Certainly not much chatter from the women. What Ray heard mostly was the rough laughter of the men. Cindy had been the only one to even interact with Ray. She was also the only one with any vitality, though she was clearly overdoing it. Body piercings, tattoos, extravagant drinking, like she was showing off how much she didn't fit in with this gang family of hers.

"No thanks," he had said crisply. "I don't drink."

"Oh come on," she had teased, "they won't see us. They won't even care. We can do whatever we want."

Ray had glanced around, noting she was right about her family's disinterest. "No thanks," he had repeated. "I don't want to. It's not whether people can see me or not, I don't want to."

Swaying on her feet, Cindy had downed another tumbler of Chardonnay. "Well, I want to," she had said. "A lot. Then I'll find someone to fuck. Maybe you. And you should know, I've been doing it a long time. If it is you, you'll get the five-star fuck of your life."

Ray had nodded with the silent poise of a bartender who listened to a lot of drunks. He knew he was looking at a bad one and didn't want her to escalate. Sinful Cindy had gone from being entertaining to unappealing in a matter of moments.

Noting his disdain, Cindy had asked: "Ray, you ever see that movie 'Pulp Fiction?'"

"Once when it first came out, crazy movie," Ray had said in a neutral tone.

"That's it. I like the black guy with the Jheri curls."

"Yeah, he's cool," Ray had agreed.

"Julius. He does all that dirty shit, but he talks cool, so he gets away with it."

"I guess that's how it works these days," Ray had said. He had noticed Cindy had stopped swaying and seemed to be gathering herself. Suddenly he knew exactly what he was looking at: Sinful Cindy was a younger, female version of what he had been in his bar fight days when he was nicknamed Wrong Way Ray.

"I'm switching to beer," she had announced, pulling four cans out of the cooler.

"Not a good idea, you'll make yourself sick," he had cautioned, faintly aware that something in her was like something still in him.

"Dude," she had said grimly, "I live sick."

Then with a manic grin, she had brightened and added: "Here's the cool thing Julius said in that movie, and I think about it all the time. Like pretty much every day." And with that, she had stepped back, cradling her four beer cans, and announced with grim purpose, "The path of the righteous one is beset on all sides by the iniquities of the selfish and the tyranny of evil men." Then she had turned, still reciting, "Blessed is she who, in the name of charity and goodwill, shepherds the weak through the valley of darkness, for she is truly her sister's keeper, and the finder of lost children." Ray went on to live a long life, but what happened next definitely became one of the wildest Big Burn funerals he would ever see. And he would go on to see a lot. Ray told it or referred to it so often that it passed into Big Burn legend.

With her family gathered around the cooker, Sinful Cindy sauntered up to the fire, ever so slightly popped open the beer cans, and finished reciting her lines, "And I will strike down upon thee with great vengeance and furious anger those who attempt to poison and destroy my daughters. And you will know my name is the Lord when I lay my vengeance upon thee!"

Then she tossed those fizzing beer cans right on the heaping pile of coals which held the last molecular remnants of her grandfather. Her family rushed over as she stared into the coals. Words were exchanged. Rebukes yelled. Cindy defiantly stood her ground beside the fire as beer sizzled and slopped all over what had been their final earthly connection with their patriarch.

Watching from the rear of the pavilion, Ray could not hear the ensuing uproar. Nor did he want to. Clearly, it was old family business — none of his concern.

An overweight, gray-haired woman in a black sweatshirt found a stick and tried to dig the hissing beer cans out of the coals. But Cindy pushed her away, and started screaming and pointing at her and the other shadowy figures in her family. You knew, you knew, was all Ray could make out Cindy screaming. Amidst a torrent of swearing, slut was the word volleyed back at her.

Cindy, pointing at the fire, pointing at the woman, waving, gesturing, crying, raged at her family until eventually, she leaned over the cooker and projectile vomited directly onto the coals.

That did it. Revulsion swept the gathering. Silent and hunched like Cro-Magnons, the family departed the fireside and returned to the campground, leaving her quite alone.

"You all right," Ray cautiously asked Cindy as he had later approached her. She was seated on a bench, face buried in her hands, weeping.

"He's burning in hell," she sobbed. "And the rest of them can go there, too. They let him do that to me. They let him do that to me. I was a child. I was their child."

Ray could hear the coals sizzling her vomit liquids into steam. The smell was ghastly. No way those commemorative ashes were worth saving. He listened to her cry for a while, then said, "Come on, I got a place you can bed down. Don't go back there with them."

He switched on a flashlight and led Cindy on the well-worn path to his yurt. As soon as they began walking, she opened up about the rapes by her grandfather. Then once they were on the dock, she went through all of it, about how her mother pretended everything was all right. Hours passed. She spoke of rape on birthdays, rape after school, on the weekends, rape with objects, pain, humiliation, shame, fear, betrayal, all washed proudly down with lots and lots of drugs, until finally the evil man had died. "I could not have asked for a better funeral than watching him burn," she said grimly. "Because I know he's burning in hell right now. I don't know why they decided to come out here and burn him up like this, but it was fucking beautiful."

And then she went to the bushes for a pee, and they fell asleep. After watching her snore for a while, Ray reached over and gave her a poke in the back. "Hey, hey, Cindy, you all right."

"Where the fuck am I?"

"Well, we're kind of camping," said Ray.

"What the fuck is all this deerskin shit?"

"It's bedding. It's how I sleep. You're out here with me and my furs because it's how I sleep."

"I'm out here camping with Daniel Boone, holy crap," Cindy sighed. She rolled over on her back and looked straight up at the breaking dawn. "Did we, you know, do anything?" she asked.

"No."

"Nothing."

"Nope."

"Damn."

"Damn."

"Oh, shit, I remember now. We talked."

"You talked. I listened."

"Right. I don't even remember your name."

"Ray."

"Hey, Ray."

"Hey."

"Thanks for this, I guess."

"Yeah."

There was a long pause. "I told you a lot of shit, didn't I?"

"You sure did."

Cindy sighed again, deeply. "I feel worse than shit."

Ray rolled over on his back and stared up at the sky. Dawn was rising over the far edge of the pond. His familiar world was coming into view. The lightening sky was cloudless, dotted yet with a smattering of morning stars. "Probably more from the drinking than the telling," he said. "But I don't think the telling was bad for you. Probably something you ought to do more often. My advice, though, is do it with someone who's not handing out drinks."

"My grandfather was evil," Cindy said in a determined tone, "He is burning in hell. I saw all that fire up around him, like it was reaching up out of the earth to pull him straight down into hell. All the shit he did to me, that's what he deserves. And they knew. They all knew. Pretended they didn't, but they did. They can all burn in hell."

"Well, from what you said he deserved to burn in hell."

"That's what I prayed for, and my prayers were answered when I saw that fire.

"I ain't much of a praying guy," said Ray, "but I don't think you can pray someone into hell. I don't think it's up to us praying to put people in hell. I don't think that's how it works."

"Oh, yeah, how does it work?"

"You can't pray someone else into hell. You can pray they fix themselves to stay out of hell, but you can't pray them into hell because God ain't listening to that prayer. God don't work that way.

God works with prayers that are worth listening to. I mean, you can wish someone into hell. But they get themselves there… or not. You ain't got nothing to do with it, and God ain't got nothing to do with

Ray paused, surprised at the conviction of his words. He had kind of thought of stuff like that before, but only ever in bits and pieces. He'd never put it all together like that.

"Well then I wished him into hell with a prayer. And it fucking worked," Cindy said bitterly.

"You may be right on that. But you got to pray yourself clean over that wish."

Ray was looking up at the sky, astonished it was him actually saying words like this, like he was some kind of preacher or something with words just coming out of him. Plus, Ray had never woke up next to a girl after a night where all he did was listen to her. This was a whole new experience for him.

"Yeah, maybe...you sound like you do a lot of praying."

"Nope, not really. I do some God talking every once in a while, but not a lot of praying. Definitely no wishing though. Wishing works about as well as playing the lottery, and I don't do either of those. I do living. That's plenty for me."

"Living," Cindy repeated sarcastically. "What the fuck is that?"

"It ain't giving up," said Ray. "Living is day by day getting it done. Better if you get it done right."

"Like my grandfather did right. Like he did right by me."

"He's dead and burned up. And if he's in hell off that, he's in hell off that. But don't let him pull you down there with him. Because guess what, he's the second grandfather who's been out here this week dead and burned up. On top of that, we've had a mom and a dad out here this week. All dead and burned up. And every single person who comes out here for these funerals we put on, when all the sadness and sorrow —"

"And hate," Cindy said, interrupting.

"And hate," agreed Ray. "And all that gets churned up in a big, crazy party, they clean up, go home and back to living. Whatever that is for them. Life goes on. Don't let it not."

Ray paused again as Cindy collected her thoughts. It was like something was unraveling inside him that was bringing these words out. No rhyme or reason to it, just tumbling out.

"Well, I sure as hell can't go back to my family," she said. "Not that I want to."

"I'd say that's true. Not after last night."

"Not after all my damn life with them."

"Look, it's your life, but it doesn't have to be a damn life. Your choice if it is or isn't. But you got to choose. You. Not them, you."

"Shit."

"Not shit. No, not shit. Look, I don't know if it was I got lucky or looked after, however you want to call it, but when my cousin got back from Iraq, I finally got it. He was in a bad way, and because of that, I realized how much he needed me. And at the same time, I was a mess, and because of that, I realized how much I needed him… his strength… his discipline. Hell, he got me this job out here. That's when I stopped being Wrong Way Ray and started being Right Way Ray. My life has been good ever since."

"So, Wrong Way Ray became Right Way Ray?"

"Just that quick, just had to change one word — wrong to right. Hell, you could do it. Change one word. You ain't got to be Sinful Cindy, hell, you could be Super Cindy."

"Super Cindy?"

"Sure, Super Cindy. After last night, I'd say you were."

"Super Cindy, huh, I like that."

Twelve

It had been a long, hot morning on the mowing tractor. It was early September in Virginia — the sun was hot, the sky was cloudless blue, and the air was dry. Just like it had been on 9/11. Ray remembered. Every time a mid-September day broke like that, he remembered.

He was taking a breather, stretching his legs, and sipping some cold water from his ice jug. He had stopped his tractor on the grassy strip beside Karen Lane, the campground road Ken had named after his deceased wife.

Ray had chosen his break spot carefully. It was right near the campground picnic pavilion and the swim beach. Most importantly, it gave him a vantage point to see Kim — well, the back of Kim's head. Her pretty, dark-haired head. She was down at the swim beach, sitting in the lifeguard chair, watching over the children. They were swimming, playing sandcastles, diving off the wood raft, or, in the case of the brave ones, jumping way up high off the rope swing.

Kim never missed a minute in that lifeguard chair. Any time there were kids out there, she was out there. Ray sipped his ice melt and thought about her, sporting her red lifeguard swimsuit like a "Baywatch" hottie, surveying the crowd, regal and serene. Out at that little campground beach, she was a sight to behold, and she knew it.

But there was more to Kim being in the lifeguard chair, a job, which Ray knew, she thoroughly enjoyed. He had never understood why until just then, but suddenly as he looked over the children at play, he understood in an all-at-once kind of way: Kim Keeney was guarding those kids for their moms.

There were a wide range of moms out there — young moms with babies and toddlers, older moms with tweens and teens, and even older moms with college kids, and watching over all of them were a couple of grandmoms, who get to be the mommiest of moms.

It was Kim's pride and joy to watch over them. Pride to watch over the kids and keep them safe. And joy to see the moms being moms. Ray had a sudden and simple understanding of Kim because he saw right there in front of her what she loved: she loved her mom, the woman who had died and left her when she was only eight years old. And watching all these women mothering their children, Ray knew, brought Kim memories of her mom, and, as well, sad glimpses of moments she and her mom had never had and would never have.

Kim Keeney loved a mom she hardly knew, and that's what Ray saw. She wasn't just a hottie, looking for a dude, though Ray was sure she was, and, further, that he was that dude. No, she was a daughter who still loved her long-dead mom in that special mother-daughter way that Ray would never, could never fully understand.

This was a different way of being for Ray, this understandingness. He wasn't really sure why it was happening, but he knew it was him being better. Something about his long, strange night with Cindy helped him see things how these girls saw themselves, more than ever before.

Something else caught Ray's eye. Besides the little kids playing in the water, there was a crew of dudes, huddled at the far end of the beach nonchalantly ogling Kim. Heck, Ray could see some of the dads were casting sly glances up her way. Nothing like being admired, he thought.

Ray smiled at the young dudes who considered themselves in Kim's league. Skinny, fish-belly pale, they didn't look strong enough to change a tire. Plus, they were goth dudes — all black clothes, city kids, definitely not for Kim.

But then who was... him?

He thought so. Never mind Big Tom's warnings against chasing Kim, Ray knew in his heart how good they'd be together. He just had to show her what was in his heart and it would work. Standing there he knew he was going to make it happen. He was Right Way Ray. Wrong Way Ray was gone. Right Way Ray was the man to make it happen.

A glance at his watch told him break time was over. He had to finish the last bit of mowing, get cleaned up, and help Big Tom heft a body to the viewing bier. They were doing it early, meaning the body would be out in the sun longer than usual. But since it would be shrouded and blanketed, no one would notice.

And apparently Big Tom really needed him because it was an extra-large lift. This big, beautiful family with all these children and moms and dads was there to cremate a big, beautiful woman. Big being the operative word for how she ended up.

Ray turned to get back on his mower and just then the rusty red catering van came bouncing down the dirt road, headed toward the campground picnic shelter to set up the campers' lunch. Only something was different. Myrna and Bev were black ladies in their fifties. This driver was a white girl. Ray could see that from a distance. And she was pretty. Ray could see that the closer she got. Real pretty, with blondish brown hair and a nice tan.

The windows on the van were rolled up to keep out the road dust, and Ray could see this pretty girl in the driver's seat was singing, like belting-it-out singing. And then just as soon as she saw Ray looking at her, she stopped singing.

And then she slowed down, like almost to a full stop. It could have been she was being respectful not to blow road dust all over him, or it could have been she was checking him out. Like seriously checking him out — and she wasn't even trying to pretend she wasn't.

By the time she pulled the van even to Ray, her driver's window was only six feet away, and she was unabashedly looking him up and down.

Ray didn't mind being ogled. In fact, he kind of liked it. She was having her own personal ladies' night with him, and all he had to do was stand there and smile and wave. He didn't even bother with his booty shake.

Apparently satisfied, she smiled and waved, and accelerated off to the picnic shelter.

Thirteen

Weirdest funeral Ray had ever seen. Twinkies everywhere. Must have been a hundred of the little, vanilla sponge cake treats unwrapped and set out on platters all around the pavilion. The family had brought them in on their own, boxes and boxes of them. Heck, there were a dozen placed on top of the shrouded body as it lay on the stretcher!

Ray was standing outside the pavilion, listening to the eulogies at the viewing bier. They were heartfelt and plentiful, and that meant the memorial service was way over schedule. That body had spent a long, hot day in the sun, even the Twinkies were wilting. It was well past time to start the burn.

The dead woman's name was Beatrice, but everyone called her Granny Bea. And they talked about her as though she was still... there — loving her children, grandchildren, great grandchildren... and her Twinkies.

Thinking he was presiding over a somber affair, Ray wore a dark button-down shirt, dress khakis, and chocolate brown desert boots. Then he saw the Twinkies. These were the folks down at the beach earlier in the day when they seemed a typical American family. But now their quirky craving was out in the open. Or was it their addiction?

Ever the supervisor, he glanced over his shoulder to check if the catering van had arrived. Not yet. Daylight was fading. Dusk was falling. But the food was still nowhere in sight. Coolers brimmed with ice and cans of beer. Trays of plastic tumblers stood at the ready by the wine casks. He had done his part, but, as of yet, the caterers were a no-show.

They got the new girl doing the delivery, thought Ray. That's what it is. And then Ray being Ray, he thought, I bet she's hot. Even in the midst of all the funeral goings on, he could picture the pretty face he had glimpsed as she drove past that morning. Best of all was recalling how she had been checking him out in a sexy way. Had to be hot.

But what was her name? She was from Vegas. He remembered that, but not her name. He had it right on the tip of his tongue. But never mind that, there were a lot of hungry guests and no food. She better get here. And soon!

Ray turned back to the funeral. Two years of helping all these families burn up their loved ones had taught him that every family had its traits. This one was no different. Their trait was quite obvious when they were all together: The girls were big and the boys were scrawny.

And Big Tom was right, it had been a very heavy stretcher. No doubt Granny Bea had lived long and well and raised a beautiful family, but along the way a lot of Twinkies had passed over her lips. Her daughters and granddaughters had followed heavily in her footsteps.

Then to Ray's experienced ears, it sounded like the eulogy speaker, a very large woman, was wrapping up. She began naming the pall-bearers and calling them out from the crowd. Good but not good. The pyre was ready to go, but where was the catering?

Ray had stationed himself halfway between the pavilion and the cooker. That way if the catering showed up before the eulogies completed, he could dart back there to help with the setup. But he was also just steps away from lighting the pyre if that came first. Again, he glanced nervously over his shoulder. And there it was! Just in time, the rusty red catering van was rattling down the driveway, dust billowing up behind it.

Way too close for comfort, thought Ray. That Vegas girl may be pretty, but Bev and Myrna need to hear about her being so late. He watched the van for a few moments, then turning his attention back to the gathering, Ray froze. The eulogies had, indeed, ended, and the pallbearers, all teenage grandkids, were already lifting the stretcher off the viewing bier. But when Ray saw how they had arranged themselves, he realized disaster was imminent: They were about to drop the body!

Every funeral supervisor's worst nightmare is a body drop, and Ray was staring right at it.

Ordinarily at Big Burn, the part of the ceremony when the pallbearers carry the body from the viewing bier to the crematorium was brief and simple. Since the distance between the two sites was only about ten yards, transferring the body between them was impossible to screw up.

But this group was different — very different. On one side of the stretcher were three big powerful girls and on the other side, three scrawny boys. And as soon as those mismatched grandkids lifted the stretcher bearing Granny Bea's extra-large body, the dignity of her funeral procession devolved to a stumbling, lurching, unforgettable mess.

Ray watched as the front corner of the stretcher dipped dangerously. The lead boy pallbearer was sagging under the load. The stretcher tipped further as the other boys buckled under the weight. In unison, all the pallbearers, boys and girls, staggered toward the cooker with the stretcher canted at a crazy forward angle. Twinkies rolled down the body like sponge cake pinballs.

For the rest of his life, as he told this story over and over, Ray Wells would insist the kid in the lead tripped over a Twinkie. "How do you trip over a Twinkie?" he'd snort. "It's a Twinkie. How does that happen?"

Immediately a collective groan rose up from the gathered family. "Watch out," screeched a big grandmother. "Don't drop her," yelled a scrawny grandfather. "Granny Bea," yelled a lucky grandkid who wasn't anywhere near that overloaded stretcher.

But it was too late. Gravity won. With the lead boy stumbling and the other two tripping over their own feet, the whole group lurched forward while simultaneously tipping the stretcher sideways. And that was when their humongous, heavy load started its slide.

It could have been worse. Granny Bea's shrouded corpse, thoroughly thawed during that warm, sunny afternoon, could have tumbled headfirst off the stretcher, hit the gravel and burst the shroud for a horrific dead-body-sprawled-out-in-full-view mess. Literally, it would have been a sight that would have haunted that family for the rest of their days. Not to mention the smell.

But it didn't happen that way. Thanks to Ray Wells.

In his baseball years, Ray had been a shortstop. He was quick with his feet and quicker with his hands. He made the catch at the front corner of the stretcher just as the body was sliding off. It was a two-handed catch. Left hand firmly grasping the front of the stretcher, right hand getting up under the shoulder to hold the body, as much as possible, from toppling off.

It was the save of a lifetime.

A quick glance at the wide-eyed pallbearers was all Ray needed to reassure them it was okay. He was there to help carry the stretcher. They were going to make it. Granny Bea wasn't going to fall. It was okay.

But in that exact instant Ray also realized HE wasn't okay because the hand he was using to support the body was gooey. Real gooey. The partial tumble off the stretcher had ripped a hole in the underside of the shroud, and his fingers had poked right through that and into the body's papery skin. So, as his left hand was grasping the stretcher, his right hand was palm-deep in back fat. Rancid, decomposing back fat.

Dead body juice, dead body juice, dead body juice, was the silent alarm sounding in Ray's head. It was a situation he had never imagined himself in, and there it was with a large, emotionally distraught family looking on.

But if there was ever a moment when Ray Wells, site supervisor for Big Burn Funeral Services, took one for the team, that was it. He kept his shortstop face implacable — grim but implacable. "Let's get her over there," he said tersely as he realized gelatinous body juices were not only coating his hand, but also dripping onto his shoes.

There was an audible sigh from the gathered family. "He's got her," came a man's voice. "They've got her," corrected a woman's voice. "Granny Bea, Granny Bea," shouted the children.

Yuck, yuck, YUCK, thought Ray, whose expression remained as focused as a slugger at the plate.

The grandkid pallbearers nodded silently as they all shuffled clumsily toward the cooker. By the looks on their faces Ray realized they couldn't see his hand. No one could. He was on the corner of the stretcher farthest from the crowd. The pallbearer kid next to him was oblivious. Ray and only Ray knew his hand was stuck inside their beloved grandmother's corpse.

We can do this, thought Ray, they don't have to know. It's a couple steps, we just got to get her there. Don't ruin the funeral. Don't ruin the funeral.

As gross as it was, Ray could see it was working. With him leading, the group would just be able to shove Granny Bea's stretcher on the cooker. They only had to get it centered so that no extremities were flopping off the side. Not a good look if there's an arm or a leg sticking out when the pyre gets lit.

Almost there, almost there, thought Ray.

And then with success just steps away, came the smell. Part pungent old food and part stinky roadkill, it wafted up as the dead body juice soaked into the underside of the shroud. The kid next to him sniffed with a grimace. Ray saw the others wrinkle their noses. "Watch that Twinkie!" he snapped. And all the pallbearer kids' heads jerked to see the sole remaining Twinkie teetering precariously at Granny Bea's feet.

Two more steps.

"Careful, careful with her," yelled a grandmother from the audience.

Then just as they centered the stretcher on the cooker, Ray with another head fake again got all the kids to simultaneously look back at Granny Bea's feet, allowing him to pull his hand free.

It was done. Disgusting and gross but done.

"All right, we made it," Ray announced loudly to the funeral procession, as he kept his hand behind his back. "Good save on that," he said to the pallbearer kids, who nodded and stepped back from the cooker with relieved expressions.

Ray had his butane lighter out in a flash. He moved quickly to light the paraffin accelerants as the family encircled the cooker at a distance of about eight feet. His shoes were ruined, and his hand was stinky with goop, but he was not yet done with his duty. With a quick wash-up, he would serve this family their drinks and supervise their after-party for as long as they needed.

The kindling caught quickly and the flames leaped up around Granny Bea's corpse. With the fire popping and crackling, all eyes were on the flames which flared ferociously — especially beneath the fat drippings. Like pouring bacon fat on a campfire, thought Ray as he backed slowly away from the cooker, goopy hand stiff at his side. The body was engulfed in flames now, the fire rising to a dramatic height. The crowd was stepping back. Sobs could be heard. A baby cried.

"She's burning. She's burning," a little girl announced in a frightened tone.

"It doesn't hurt, Granny Bea, does it?" a second little girl wondered aloud.

"No, honey," said her daddy. "Granny Bea doesn't feel that. She's already in heaven. It's just her Earth body burning, and then it goes up to God in that smoke. Granny Bea's soul is already there, with him up in heaven."

Whew. It was done. But a quick glance in the pavilion told Ray the catering still wasn't set out. The van was there. He'd seen it arrive, but where the heck was the catering. In all the excitement of getting Granny Bea's body safely onto the cooker, he'd lost track of time. And now on top of him having the grossest hand in the history of the world, the catering still wasn't done.

Ray hustled toward the empty pavilion, hand dangling at his side. He was marching straight for the sink near the wine bar, where he could thankfully wash that dead body juice off his hand, when around the corner and straight into his path walked the most beautiful girl he had ever seen.

She was a living, breathing angel. Tan and healthy — brownish-blonde hair, cute bob haircut framing her pretty face, generous smile, piercing deep green eyes, and curves — toned curves in all the right places. She was wearing a tight grey sweatshirt with cutoff sleeves, a short blue jean skirt, and Birkenstocks.

And as he beheld her, Ray Wells, site supervisor for Big Burn Funeral Services, did what any man would do, he stopped, frozen in place with an expression of wonder on his face, like a tourist gaping at Michelangelo's masterpiece on the ceiling of the Sistine Chapel.

"Hi, I'm Bonnie — Bonnie Betts," she announced as she stepped confidently toward him with her right hand outstretched. "You must be Ray."

It was a simple handshake this beautiful young woman was offering, the most basic element of civility, but right there, in that moment, Ray Wells, the cockiest ladies' man in the county, was stuck like a fly in a web.

As she saw it, he had nothing in his hands. Obviously he should respond immediately and shake hers. With a large picnic basket in her left hand, she held her right out for him. It was a normal, natural, professional gesture. She was offering him her hand, he should accept. He should welcome her without hesitation to the Big Burn — to show his respect and approval of her, to connect with her physically, to certify the promise of their future, all which he desperately wanted to do.

But he couldn't.

Because it was his RIGHT hand that was covered in rancid dead body juice. And shaking hands with Bonnie just then would be him spreading it on her.

Yuck.

But it wasn't just inexplicable, it was insulting. If he didn't shake her hand right then and there, she would think he had spurned her invitation. Her first impression would be one of discomfort and distrust, an immediate loss of goodwill. An epic fail between them.

Washing wasn't a good option either. She was waiting, hand outstretched, the moment was now. So Ray did what any red-blooded, virile man would do when faced with a chance to impress a pretty girl — he faked it as best he could. Quick as a blink, he wiped his hand on the backside of his best pair of pants and shook Bonnie's hand with a firm grip and a warm, buttery smile. "Hi, I'm Ray Wells," he said. "Welcome to Big Burn."

Bonnie smiled and nodded, giving Ray just the slightest reassuring squeeze, and in that moment, when she looked up into his eyes, he knew he'd done the right thing.

"Hi, Ray," she said. "I've heard a lot about you." Then with a wrinkled brow she queried, "What's with all the Twinkies?"

"Let me jump over to this sink for a second," he said. "I just lit up the pyre and want to wash my hands."

"Oh, right," said Bonnie. "Oh my gosh, look at that fire. It's huge. Did you put gasoline on it?" she asked.

Ray followed her arm gesturing toward the pyre, which was now roaring up around Granny Bea's corpse. The swirling flames so intense, her shrouded body was literally melting into them. "No, we don't use gasoline," he said as he bent over the sink and washed and washed and washed his hands.

All the while Bonnie stood staring, transfixed at the sight of extremely obese human remains being immolated in a towering bonfire as a large gathering of mourners looked on in silence.

Finally, with his hands hospital clean and thoroughly dried with paper towels, Ray joined her. She had gone to the front of the pavilion where she could see the ever growing flames. "I have never seen such a huge fire. Whatever is making it burn like that?"

"Twinkies," Ray said softly. "Twinkies."

"Wow," she said not taking her eyes from the sight.

The huge blaze cast its orange glow far up in the pavilion. Shadow and light flickered off the walls and ceiling in the gathering dusk. Ray Wells, standing next to Bonnie Betts, studied the lines of her face.

"Wow is right," he repeated.

Fourteen

"Bonnie's young," said Ken.

"Oh," said Ray.

"She's only twenty," said Ken.

"What!" Ray just about dropped his sun tea. "She's only twenty!"

Ray and Ken were side by side, leaning back on the tailgate of Ken's truck. Each had a jar of sun tea, cold from the kitchen fridge. Ken had come out to check on Ray and he'd brought quenchers.

"Yeah, twenty — but she acts older. Her mom died, and she's been living on her own in Vegas for a couple years," said Ken.

"Huh, on her own in Vegas," said Ray, recovering his composure. There was a protectiveness to Ken's tone, and Ray decided to refrain from commenting on the idea of a teenage hottie "on her own" in Vegas.

Ken, for his part, was watching Ray for a clue of his thinking about Bonnie. Finally, he changed the subject. "Big Tom tells me it got a bit messy for you last night," he said.

"Yeah, it did," said Ray with a shudder. "I'll never forget that smell, and I'll never eat another Twinkie. I had to throw away my clothes and shoes."

"I heard," said Ken. "That's not something you should pay for, so go ahead and buy yourself some new ones, just turn the receipt in to Kim, she'll reimburse you out of petty cash."

"That would be awesome," said Ray. "Thanks, Ken."

"You bet," said Ken. "I got to take care of my crew. You guys are working hard and doing a good job. We keep at it, and I think Big Burn has got a big future."

They were on the road near the memorial garden. It was mid-September. Ray had just finished planting and watering the deer-proof shrubs he had trucked in from the nursery in Charlottesville. His boots, jeans, and T-shirt were mud-spattered. It had been a messy job for Ray to do alone, but he bore down and got it done. Big Tom had taken another morning off to meet with Kelly and the midwife.

Ken had caught up to Ray at the end of the job, as he had been sweeping deer poo off the "fancy path." A quick talk over sun tea while leaning on Ken's tailgate was all the business conference they needed.

"Hey, look, there's that buck," said Ray, as he watched the whitetail with massive antlers stroll into view. The giant male was cautiously following a trio of does as they emerged from a clump of head-high white pines.

"Yup," said Ken, "there he is, Old Methuselah. I haven't seen him for a good while."

"That's what you call him?"

"Yeah, Methuselah. I first saw him after Karen died, about twenty years now. He was big then. He's just gotten bigger and bigger."
"Old Methuselah, huh?"

"Yeah, what do you call him?"

"Big Fucking Buck."

Ken laughed. "Yeah, he is that. He and his does. I think they smell those new plants you just put out."

"Right there in their bedroom, yeah, probably."

The does moved nonchalantly amongst the rows of maturing Christmas trees that formed the backdrop for Kim's memorial garden. They were feeding on the knee-high grass and wildflowers that grew there. The big buck hung back, watching.

"A lot of folks would love to get that rack on their wall," said Ray.

"Yeah, they would," agreed Ken. "But they won't get him. Ain't no one taking him off this farm. He's our buck."

"Spirit animal," said Ray.

"Spirit animal," echoed Ken, taking a pull on his Mason jar. "He absolutely is." And for a few moments both men fell silent as they watched the buck finally drop his head to feed.

"So, hey, Ray, on a serious note," said Ken, "Tom and I are off to Florida tomorrow. We're going to be scouting some new locations for expansion, be gone about a week. I'm counting on you to handle things here while we're gone."

Ken was looking Ray right in the eye, man to man. Something about the way he was being addressed made Ray feel like he had just hit one over the fence. "Okay," was all he said.

"Kimmy can handle the bookings, the arrivals, and the record-keeping. You just got to keep things running smooth day-to-day with the campground and the cremations. Think you can do that for a week or so without me and Big Tom?"

"Yeah, no problem," said Ray. "I mean, it will be a little hectic."

"I understand," Ken interjected. "Kelly is going to help, too. She can fill in for some of Big Tom's stuff, as long as you show her what she needs to do. Can you do that?"

"Sure," Ray said agreeably. "Kelly will do great. And she's getting big with the baby coming. I can do whatever lifting and moving stuff needs to be done. Hopefully we won't have any more extra-large bodies for a while."

"We'll see," said Ken. "And also Bonnie is going to come and help Kelly and kind of work her way in with us."

"Bonnie?"

"Yeah, Bonnie," repeated Ken.

"I thought she was with Bev and Myrna."

"She is," Ken added quickly. "But I think it's better if she works it from our side, like based with us and doing catering runs from here. She has her little car that she drove here, but she'll use my truck for the catering runs. All Bev and Myrna got to worry about is cooking. And that way Bonnie can onboard with us."

"Bonnie is with us?"

"Yeah, Bonnie is with us. And she's going to move in with Kelly and Tom, to help Kelly around the house while Tom is down in Florida with me. She might even stay in there with them until Kelly delivers."

"Oh, wow."

"Yeah, and apparently they are going to plan the baby's room together."

Ray chuckled, "Definitely don't need Tom for that," he said.

"No, they don't," agreed Ken. "I think that will work out real well with her and Kelly. They're bonding over the religion thing."

"The religion thing?" asked Ray.

"Yeah, well, Bonnie has gotten real religiousy all of a sudden. I knew her growing up, her and her mom. I'd go out and visit them in Vegas every year, and they weren't all that religiousy then. But now all of sudden Bonnie calls herself a Jesus girl."

"A Jesus girl? Bonnie is a Jesus girl?"

"By way of Vegas, yeah."

Ray thought for a moment about how Vegas, a place he'd never been to, and Jesus, a Bible guy he'd never seen, had combined to give that pretty girl a warm and genuine smile. "Well, I mean, that's good for her and Kelly," said Ray. "Kelly's a church girl. She's strong with that. She sure got Big Tom pulled in there with her."

"Kelly will definitely be a good influence for Bonnie," agreed Ken. "And Bonnie can definitely help Kelly get ready for the baby. Bonnie has got some growing up to do, and this will be a good place for her to do it."

Ray scratched his chin. "Yeah, this will be a good place for her," he said.

"And, Ray," said Ken, shifting to a serious tone, "you got to promise me you're there for her, too. She's a good kid. It's important we help her be a good kid. You behave yourself. Don't get yourself stirred up with her. Just give her some space." Ken was looking Ray right in the eye. "Promise me, Ray," he repeated.

"I promise," said Ray, returning his gaze. "Ken, you ain't got to worry about me and Bonnie."

Fifteen

"I found Jesus in Des Moines," said Bonnie, her voice lilting like a child who had discovered a bird's nest filled with eggs. "He was on the radio, talking to me. Well, actually it was a preacher, but right then and there, I knew it was Jesus who was talking to me through that preacher."

"Des Moines, huh?" said Ray, over his shoulder. He was leading Bonnie into Walk-in Number One, where they stored the bodies scheduled for imminent cremation. Walk-in Number Two was the refrigerator where the new arrivals began their two-week wait.

They were in the Metal Barn, the metal building Ken had built on a hunch three years earlier. A modestly successful Christmas tree farmer, he had mortgaged a big chunk of his family's heritage on the idea that Americans wanted more freedom of expression in their funerals. "You want to sell something in America, make it about freedom," he said.

And he was right. The bureaucracy around funerals was excessive. Ken knew in his gut families wanted a final goodbye that was intimate and informal. Not to mention less expensive. The more people found out about it, the more people realized Ken Keeney's Big Burn Family Funeral was a godsend.

But as demand for Big Burn pyre cremations had skyrocketed, so had the workflow. Now with the second walk-in, additional supply storage shelves, and the crusher, the hydraulic press Big Tom used to pulverize the teeth and bone fragments, the Metal Barn was the busiest building on the farm.

"Yes, Des Moines," continued Bonnie, barely pausing to catch her breath. She didn't seem at all concerned by the prospect of seeing a refrigerator filled with dead bodies. "Oh, it was so pretty there. It was a bright, sunny day and all the corn was so tall and green and beautiful. And I was feeling scared and lonely, like I was living a terrible mistake of a life. And then the Word of God came to me right as I was driving down the highway through miles and miles of that corn. As long as I live, I'll never forget that moment — never, never, never. I was just driving along, surrounded by beautiful green life everlasting, and Jesus was filling my heart with the joy of the Holy Spirit."

Ray had stopped at the walk-in door and was patiently hearing Bonnie out. When she stopped, he tapped the door. "This is Walk-in Number One," he said, in an instructive tone. "We got four bodies in here on bunk beds. Well, I call them bunk beds. They're just big metal shelves, but I like to think of them as bunk beds since they're laying down."

"Are they just laying there, like..." Bonnie finished her question with a wince.

"In body bags," said Ray. "Always in body bags. When Kim picks them up, they go in one of our body bags. And we don't take them out until Kelly does prep and shroud, which is what she's going to show you how to do now."

"Do you do prep and shroud?" Bonnie asked.

"Who, me?" chuckled Ray. "No, I do just about everything else out here, but I don't do prep and shroud."

"He's scared," Kelly called out, grinning. She was across the room, standing next to the prep table, a waist-high wooden platform topped with grey Formica. She was pulling a paper surgical apron over her farm clothes. Her maternity top and maternity jeans were stretched tight over her belly.

"I ain't scared," protested Ray. "I just don't like seeing them when they come out of the bag. It gives me the heebies."

"We'll all be like that someday," said Kelly, with a hint of her native Texas twang. She was a tall, straight-backed woman with dark brown hair, walnut brown eyes, and a ready smile. On her thin frame, her pregnant belly was quite pronounced. "Hopefully, when it happens, we'll be treated with respect."

"But I thought Kim did the marketing and the office work," chirped Bonnie.

Now it was Ray's turn to wince. "Huh?"

"You said you do just about everything else out here, but I thought Kim did the marketing and office work, at least that's what she told me," said Bonnie.

"Well, yes, she does," admitted Ray.

"Okay, so when you say you do 'just about everything else out here,' there's a teeny bit of exaggeration in there?" she asked.

Kelly laughed. Ray smiled. Bonnie was grinning in a pretty girl kind of way that he did not want to argue with. "Okay," he said, "maybe not everything else, but a lot of it."

"Ray is definitely in charge of the department of exaggeration here at Big Burn," laughed Kelly.

"I never would have guessed," teased Bonnie.

Ray gave Bonnie a tolerant smile. He opened the refrigerator door and switched on the interior light. "Walk-in Number One," he said. "You go first and find the toe tag marked Goldner."

Then to make sure, he called over his shoulder: "Goldner, right, Kel?"

"Goldner, yes, we're prepping Goldner," Kelly called back.

"Okay, go all the way in, find the Goldner toe tag. You take the end with the feet, which is the easy end. We keep the heads towards the door, that's the heavy end. I'll grab that."

Bonnie moved quickly into the walk-in. Ray followed. The body bag was constructed of sturdy vinyl-coated canvas. It had grab loop handles at either end. The body was of a thin elderly woman, an easy carry. In a matter of moments, they had placed the bag on the prep table in front of Kelly, who had by now donned a paper surgical mask and yellow rubber kitchen gloves.

"Those are for you," Kelly indicated a green, paper hospital apron, a disposable, blue face mask, and yellow rubber gloves she had set at the far end of the prep table for Bonnie.

"We're very gentle here," Kelly explained. "And very basic. No sawing or cutting or draining or sewing. We just wash and anoint and wrap. Kind of what the women were going to do for Jesus on Easter Sunday when they found the empty tomb."

"Hey, yeah," Bonnie said eagerly. "We're kind of like those Bible ladies helping Jesus."

"Exactly," said Kelly. "Exactly. We do this with respect and, well, even love — I think of it like the way I loved my dolls when I did their dress-up. Even though they couldn't talk to me, I knew they appreciated that I was caring for them."

"Oh, I know what you mean," said Bonnie.

Ray nodded along. Bonnie had a sunny disposition, but the hard part was still to come.

On the table near Kelly was a neat stack of thin cotton bedsheets. "We go through more sheets than a hospital," she said. "We buy them in bulk and burn them up two at a time."

Next to the sheets was a bundle of wooden barbecue skewers. There was also a large metal bowl filled with sudsy water. Two shower sponges were floating in it. A smaller basin of what appeared to be vegetable oil was also at hand, as was a roll of paper towels and a white plastic garbage bag.

"Bonnie, go ahead and gown up," instructed Kelly.

As Bonnie donned the paper apron, mask, and gloves, Kelly said, "Ray, give me a hand here."

Ray, wearing just his farm clothes, went to the foot end of the Goldner body bag as Kelly unzipped it. Then Kelly spread a bedsheet flat out on the prep table, turning it to a diamond configuration. Ray and Kelly tipped the body out face-down on it and arranged it in the center axis of the diamond. Ray took the body bag and put it in a hamper in the corner near the washing machine.

Bonnie was momentarily speechless as she watched Kelly drape the body's rear end with the still folded second sheet. "Just going to protect her modesty," said Kelly.

"Oh, my, look at those scars on her back," exclaimed Bonnie.

"Yeah," said Kelly. "Poor dear. She was an Army nurse in Vietnam. I wonder if it was from something that happened over there. The brothers told Kim her cancer was from Agent Orange."

Bonnie stood, rooted in place, as if pondering for the first time what she was about to do. "Ready?" Kelly asked.

"I guess so," Bonnie replied sheepishly, as she followed Kelly's example and picked up a sponge. "You staying over there, Ray?"

"Right where I am," said Ray, who had settled in the chair by the hydraulic press.

With Kelly silently demonstrating, she and Bonnie sponged the dead woman's neck, back, and legs in a kind of hush. "It's weird that she's cold," murmured Bonnie. "Should we pray for her?"

"I say a prayer to myself for the families to be at peace," said Kelly. "Kind of like my version of a condolence card. But that's as far as I go. Religion is so personal. I don't cross the wires between my religion and theirs. That's not our role here."

Bonnie nodded.

After the sponge bath, Kelly and Bonnie anointed the body's neck, back, and legs with paper towels infused with the cleansing oil. "Smells fresh, like a pine forest," said Kelly. "It's jojoba with a few drops of essential oil of spruce. It helps. Sometimes people are so distraught they bury their face in the shroud."

"Oh, gosh," whispered Bonnie. "I can imagine. I remember for my mom, I hardly realized the urn they gave me was her. I was like, where is she?"

Kelly nodded, then removed the folded sheet that served as the modesty drape. "Okay, let's roll her," she said.

Bonnie looked briefly at the woman's face. Ten days of refrigerated death was not what she had expected. She looked quickly away.

"You get used to it," Kelly said gently. "No job is perfect."

Kelly draped the dead woman's privates with the folded sheet, then she and Bonnie sponged her neck, midriff, legs, feet, and then applied the oil. "Okay, now we start wrapping the shroud," said Kelly. "Grab a couple skewers."

Removing the folded sheet from the woman's privates, Kelly pulled the sheet corners up over the head, feet and torso, and fastened them tight along the belly with the wooden skewers. Bonnie saw how the body silhouetted under the sheer, single sheet needed more coverage. Kelly spread the second sheet out on the table and turned it to a diamond configuration. Then she and Bonnie rolled the dead woman over face-down on that. They gathered the corners of the second sheet and fastened them tight along the spine with wooden skewers.

"There," said Kelly. "Two sheets is enough for dignity. Three is too bulky."

"And expensive," added Ray, who, now that the body was shrouded, had joined the two women at the prep table. He slid a lashed-up, wooden stretcher up on the table beside the body.

"And expensive," agreed Kelly. "But mostly it's because they become just a lump of sheets. With two, you still see their profile, and that's a comfort for the family."

They rolled the tightly shrouded body face-up onto the stretcher. It was now ready for the pyre. Next stop was the back of the hearse for a ride to the viewing bier, followed shortly thereafter by the family's commemoration, and, of course, cremation on the pyre.

"What do you think, Bonnie? It's not so terrible, is it?"

"No, actually it's not. It helps to think of it as dressing up one of my dolls."

"Good," said Kelly. "I think of it as my small contribution to their end-of-life dignity. And it's definitely better to have someone helping."

"I can't imagine being in a funeral home where they do the embalming with all those chemicals and such," said Bonnie. "This seems so much more, I don't know, kind."

"We like to think so," said Kelly. "The families certainly do. Then they go out and celebrate in the after-party."

"All different kind of ways," said Ray.

"For instance," said Kelly, "since this lady is a veteran, and her family has given us a flag, we're going to do a flag drape. Ray, it's in that brown bag over by my purse. Can you bring that over?"

Ray retrieved the brown bag and handed it to Kelly. Inside it was a Stars and Stripes flag folded triangle-style. She unwrapped it and laid it over the body, with the Stars over the head.

"Are they going to burn it?" asked Bonnie.

"No," said Kelly. "Kim told me the brothers are going to fold it up and hand it to the grandkids."

"Oh," said Bonnie, relieved.

"Yeah, then I light the pyre," said Ray. "We do a lot of veteran cremations, probably one every two weeks or so. And if they get a flag drape, we don't put the Big Burn body blanket on them."

"Oh, my," said Kelly. "That baby is kicking up a storm just now."

"Really?" gushed Bonnie, taking off her gloves. "Let me feel."

Kelly peeled off her paper gown. Lifting up the bottom edge of her maternity top, she placed Bonnie's hand at the lower end of her tight-as-a-watermelon belly.

"Oh, my goodness," squealed Bonnie. "Those are big kicks. Do you think it's a boy?"

"Well, Tom is sure hoping for a boy, but I think she's a girl. I have a strong feeling about her being a her. Every time I feel her kick, I think her. I think that's her telling her me she's a girl."

Ray was quietly enjoying the conversation. He knew how excited Big Tom was to be a dad.

"Ray, come and feel this little baby wiggling around in there," said Bonnie, who grabbed Ray's big, calloused hand and placed it on Kelly's bare belly. Kelly smiled as Ray gently laid his hand atop her rounded midriff. "Wow," was all he could say.

Ray had never so much as touched a pregnant woman before. And now he was palming Kelly's basketball of a belly, feeling the faint flutters as the baby kicked. Ray smiled that those tiny legs had so much life in them! He had always trusted Kelly's intuition. In his mind he could picture her with a baby girl, just as she had said. And with Kelly and Big Tom as her parents, that little baby was going to be one tough little girl. He'd be her Uncle Ray, teach her how to fish, maybe even hunt. Uncle Ray.

Some moments at work were better than others. Just then Ray Wells, site supervisor for Big Burn Funeral Services, was having a good one. He was in the presence of four women — one dead, a hero to her nation, and about to be cremated in front of her family; two lively, lovely ladies giggling over plans to decorate a baby's room; and a teeny tiny little one kicking up a storm in her mother's womb.

"Circle of life," thought Ray Wells. "Circle of life."

Sixteen

"Ray, is there something you want to tell me about that sweaty handshake you gave me the other day?" asked Bonnie.

"What do you mean?"

Ray and Bonnie were in the Big Burn "hearse," which Ray found himself driving for the first time ever because for some reason Kim had shirked her responsibility of transporting the shrouded Goldner body to the viewing bier.

When Ken had first pitched Kim on his idea of burning up dead people in funeral pyres and having her drive the hearse, she had demanded an Escalade with tinted windows. He'd agreed and ordered one with a large cargo deck. But it took having Big Burn Funeral Services painted on the side doors in elegant cursive writing before the whole package had enough class and prestige to bring Kim fully on board. She then declared it her vehicle, meaning only she drove it.

"That sweaty handshake we had from that night with the Twinkie people, when we first met," said Bonnie.

"Dead body juice," Ray said flatly.

"What?"

"Dead body juice from the Twinkie lady."

"Dead body juice, are you kidding me?"

"Wish I was," Ray said with a grimace. "Poked my hand inside her shoulder by mistake, and, well, yuck."

"Oh, yuck is right."

"Yeah, sorry about that. I had to throw my shoes and pants away. I wiped my hand off as best I could, but, yeah, it was still a little goopy."

Bonnie was staring straight ahead through the windshield. "Well, thank you for telling me," she said. "I appreciate you being honest about it."

"Yeah, you had your hand out, and I didn't want to be awkward because you're so damn pretty."

"Oh," said Bonnie, brightening. "That's nice… I think."

"Well, it's the truth, and I'll always tell you the truth. Like it or not. Just easier that way."

Bonnie nodded. "That's good to know, Ray." She paused for a moment, looking off to the wooded mountains rising in the distance. "It's so green here," she said.

"Well, yeah, it's the Blue Ridge," said Ray. "And we've been having a good year with rain. The fall colors are on the way. These mountains will be the prettiest place on Earth in a few weeks."

"I mean, Vegas is so brown," said Bonnie. "Well, once you get out of town. Because it's all desert. Everywhere you go, it's all brown and dry."

"Yeah, Virginia ain't Vegas," chuckled Ray. "This is a big deal, me driving this," he added. "Transporting bodies is usually Kim's job, mostly because she won't let anyone else touch the Escalade."

"But here we are," said Bonnie, switching around the radio dial. She stopped at a station playing a song about God's country.

"But here we are," echoed Ray.

"I think Kim is indisposed," said Bonnie. "Last I saw she was down at the beach, talking to a cute guy. He was buzzing around her lifeguard chair like a fly on honey."

"A guest?" asked Ray.

"Yes, a guest," said Bonnie. "Almost the entire time I was down there for lunch, they were one-on-one, in their own little world."

"That's crazy," said Ray.

"Why?" Bonnie asked, with a bit of defiance. "Why is it crazy for a pretty girl to talk to a cute guy?"

Ray, noting Bonnie's tone, kept his eyes on the dusty gravel road. "No, I mean, Kim can talk to anybody she wants to," Ray said hurriedly. "But she never wants to, at least not so far. She's always been kind of stuck up about the people who come out here for our funerals. And she's the one who recruits them, but then she doesn't have much to do with them after that. I'm just surprised she's actually talking to a guest."

"Well, I saw him in his Speedo, so I'm not at all surprised she was talking to him because he was one fine looking man."

"Speedo," Ray harrumphed.

Bonnie laughed. "If I didn't know better, I'd say you were a little bit jealous there, Mr. Ray Wells."

"Cutoffs is all you need."

"Or just plain old birthday suit."

"What do you mean?"

"I heard about you and your skinny dipping —" Bonnie paused for effect — "activities."

Ray stared straight ahead, not sure what to say.

"Yes, Ray, I know about your tipi and your Indian grandmother. Uh-huh, all that."

"From Kelly or Tom?"

"Both. Tom warned me about you."

"Oh, yeah, what did he say?"

"He said, watch out."

"What did you say?"

"I said, 'Tom, I was a cocktail waitress in Vegas strip club when I was seventeen. I know what I'm doing.'"

Ray's eyes bugged out. "Strip club?" he gasped with a hopeful sideways glance.

"Put your eyes back in, Froggy," Bonnie laughed. "Yes, strip club, The Garden, to be exact. I'll tell you about it later."

"Well, if you don't, you know I'm asking. The Garden, huh?"
"The Garden," said Bonnie.

They arrived at the viewing bier, and Ray parked. "Guests will be arriving in three hours, but we're basically ready now. I've already set the logs in the cooker. The pyre is done," he said. "We'll move the body to the bier. And then you can head out for the catering run while I set up for the party."

"That's good," said Bonnie. "Bev and Myrna said they'd have everything ready for me."

After they had placed the flag-draped stretcher on the viewing bier, Ray led Bonnie up to the pavilion. "I put the beer coolers in the back of Ken's truck. Kelly is driving them down. They're iced and ready. I just got to set them out. You guys can switch vehicles. She'll take the hearse back to the house. You can take the truck to Bev and Myrna's, and then come back with the food."

"Sounds like a plan," said Bonnie.

"I don't know where Kim is," huffed Ray, "but we could sure use her help."

Just then Kim — not Kelly — pulled up in Ken's pickup truck. And when she climbed out of the driver's seat, Ray's jaw dropped. Kim was all freshened up and wearing what looked like an Aussie Outback outfit, complete with her Lady Akubra hat. "Change of plan," she chirped.

"What?" said Ray.

"I'm doing the after-party."

"You want to do the after-party?"

"Yes, and I brought the tinnies."

"Tinnies?" asked Ray.

"Tinnies," Kim replied haughtily. "It's what they call beer cans in Australia. That's what Anthony told me."

"Anthony?" said Ray.

"Yes, Anthony. He's my mate. G'day, mate," she chirped, imitating an Aussie accent.

Kim was practically giddy in a way Ray had never seen. "Ray, I'll light the pyre and do the party," she said. "You guys just help me set up, then you can go."

"You're going to do it all?" asked Ray in a skeptical tone.

"Yes, I am," said Kim. "I got everything in the truck. Beer coolers and the catering. I picked it up already, and I sent Kelly home early. Once everything is ready to go here, it's my show. You guys help with setup, drive the truck back, and leave me the Escalade."

"You sure you can handle them if they get, you know, enthusiastic?" asked Ray.

"I'll be fine," said Kim. "They're a small group, only about twenty guests. Anthony will be there. He can help me. It was his idea. It's his aunt who died. He came all the way from Australia for her funeral. He wants me to meet this side of his family. There's a bunch of them who live Down Under, but he was the only one to make the trip for the funeral."

"Ooh, girl," squealed Bonnie. "Meeting his family. That's huge. You look great. They're going to love you."

"Oh, thank you," cooed Kim. "I'm kind of excited."

"Anthony from Australia," said Ray.

"Anthony from Australia," said Kim. "Well, actually, he's from Tasmania."

"Tasmania!" exclaimed Bonnie. "Wait, that's in Australia?"

"Yes, it's part of Australia."

"Here's me thinking that was way out in the middle of the ocean by Gilligan's Island."

"Me, too," said Ray, "but with ferocious slobbery animals whirling around on it."

Kim laughed. "That's what I thought, too. But no, it's part of Australia. Anthony says it's a lot like Virginia. He's a casino guy. He runs a casino there."

"Oh, honey, a casino guy," said Bonnie, raising her eyebrows. "I've known more than my share. Be careful."

Kim forced a smile as though holding back a reply. "Help me set this up, and you guys can go," was all she said.

Seventeen

"Turn around, Ray," called out Bonnie. "Don't look. You promised you wouldn't."

Ray Wells, site supervisor for Big Burn Funeral Services, was treading water. He was ten feet off the dock he had built at "his end" of the swim lake on the Keeney Family Farm. He was naked from head to toe. Every item of clothing he had been wearing seconds before — boots, socks, T-shirt, work jeans, underwear — lay scattered across the dock as though he'd ripped it off his body in a frenzy.

That would have been true. And the fact that Bonnie Betts was standing in the center of Ray's clothing eruption indicated that she had been in close proximity of him undressing. Only, she was not naked. At least not yet. Nor was she anywhere near as enthusiastic about stripping off as Ray had been.

"Come on in," said Ray. "The water is great."

"Oh, I'm sure it is, but you have to turn around. You promised."

"I said I won't look, and I won't," coaxed Ray. "But you sure were looking at me when I was."

Bonnie giggled. "Yes, I was, Ray Wells," she said. "And I must say I was veeeery impressed. But I certainly don't know why you are so excited. It's just little old me getting undressed. Believe it or not, I do it every day. Here, I'll step out of my sandals."

And, smiling at Ray like she was putting on a show, Bonnie lithely kicked off her Birkenstocks. Ray, also smiling, swam closer for a better view.

Bonnie then went over to the edge of the dock and daintily dipped a toe in. "Oh, that's lovely," she purred. "Is it lovely, Ray? So inviting."

"Yes, it is," said Ray with every ounce of encouragement he could muster. "Very lovely, very inviting. Keep going now."

"Oh, I will," said Bonnie. "I'm just, you know, enjoying the moment." And she beamed a big inviting smile at Ray.

"Yeah, me, too," Ray said quickly. "And I'll be enjoying it a whole lot more when you jump in. Then we can be together. That's when the fun really starts."

Bonnie gave Ray a saucy wink, unbuttoned her blue jean skirt, slid it off over her bare feet, and stepped out of it. At the sight of Bonnie wearing lacy black panties and a tan polo shirt, Ray went silent. Gulpingly silent.

Bonnie smiled as she folded her jean skirt. "Okay, Ray, now turn around," she said in a sing-song voice. "Because that's what you promised."

"Well, yes, Miss Betts, while I did promise not to look when we're swimming," Ray replied, trying to sound lawyerly, "I didn't say anything about me having a peek while you're taking your clothes off to GO swimming."

Bonnie giggled again. "Oh, Mr. Wells," she said in mock exasperation. "You are so clever. I just have no choice but to be awed by your cleverness."

Raising her arms above her head so her shirt shifted upward, just above her belly button, Bonnie gave a little twirl. Ray gaped in stupefied silence. Lacy black panties, taut and toned body, she had him at full attention.

"There," she said. "That's all the show I'm going to give you. Now turn around and don't peek. Come on. Do as I say."

"Fine," said Ray. "I'll close my eyes." And he squinted with his eyes closed just enough so he could peek through his eyelashes.

Bonnie giggled and said in a tone of mock indignation, "Ray Wells, you must think I'm the little girl who is going behind the garage to take her underwear off just because you say so. You need to turn around."

Ray laughed, but did not comply. He just stayed treading water, squinting as though his eyes were closed.

With a lift of her chin, Bonnie said, "I know your sort." And then turning her back to Ray while still well covered by her shirttail, she slipped off her panties.

Ray, still pretending his eyes were closed, craned his neck, and swam a few more strokes toward the dock. Bonnie's polo shirt had become a short dress, a very short dress, but just long enough to cover everything Ray wanted to admire. "You wearing a bras under that shirt?" he asked.

"Now why would I do that?" replied Bonnie. "And I thought you said your eyes were closed."

"Must be really hot in that shirt," purred Ray. "This water is so cool and inviting."

"Ray Wells, I can see you are keenly interested in me removing my shirt," teased Bonnie, shaking a finger at Ray, "but it is time you do as you promised and turn around."

Silently, pretending reluctance, Ray Wells spun himself so his back was to the dock. Seeing that, Bonnie whipped her polo shirt over her head, dropped it on the dock on top of her sandals, skirt, and panties, and dived a shallow dive into the pond, angling her entry so she surfaced several feet away from Ray.

Big wet smile, hair plastered back around her pretty face, Bonnie Betts, assistant to the director for Big Burn Funeral Services, was now fully nude and treading water mere yards away from her supervisor, Ray Wells.

"There you are," he crowed triumphantly. "Welcome to the deep end. You sure look pretty."

"Thank you, Ray," Bonnie said sweetly. "And thank you for inviting me to go skinny dipping so you could see me naked."

"Well, I ain't seen you naked yet," said Ray.

"Well, no, you haven't, have you?" said Bonnie, who was swimming a breaststroke with her head above the water.

Like most spring-fed, farm ponds, the Keeney farm pond was naturally clean, though somewhat murky. From the distance between them, Ray could see Bonnie's head and face, and that was all. The only way for him to get a full body view would be to swim right up next to her.

Ray Wells had never been one to hide his intentions with his skinny dipping companions, and so, with a broad, cheeky grin, he did just that, swimming a lifeguard stroke straight for Bonnie, keeping his head above water and never taking his eyes off her.

Giggling, Bonnie let him approach to within a few feet, and then she dipped under the surface and darted off to the side. Ray laughed and pursued her, only to watch helplessly as each time he got close to her she easily eluded him. All he ever saw of her was her feet splashing water at him as she kicked away.

"Hey," he said, with a hint of exasperation.

"Hey," she replied innocently.

"Let's swim together."

"We are, Ray. And I must say, I am thoroughly enjoying being out here skinny dipping with you on this lovely evening."

"Well, we could make it lovelier if we swam up close with each other. You know, together."

"Oh, really?"

"Yes, really. You know, just kind of rubbing up against each other like a couple of dolphins."

"Sexy freshwater dolphins, Ray?"

"Damn," Ray slapped at the water in frustration. "Big Tom told you that, too, didn't he?"

"Yes, he did, Ray," said Bonnie triumphantly. "And he told me about the piggybacking, and the fur pile, and your—" at this Bonnie paused for effect — "abode."

Ray, treading water, sighed deeply. "He must really like you."

"He does. Kelly does, too. I feel like she's my long lost sister. I never had a sister, and now, thanks to Jesus, I have her in my life. Well, I have both of them in my life."

"Damn," Ray said again, then with an impish grin, he added, "So you want to go piggybacking and see my... abode?"

Bonnie laughed. "You are such a funny man," she said. "But, no, Ray, I don't want to go see your... abode."

"Piggybacking?"

"No, not tonight."

"Naked dolphin swimming?"

"No, that's not a good idea either, at least for tonight. Maybe later. But we'll see how it goes."

"Well, then what are we doing out here?"

"Skinny dipping, and that's all." Now it was Bonnie's turn for an impish grin. "Well, almost all."

"What do you mean 'almost?'" Ray asked, matching her grin for grin.

"Almost means we are going to do something else, and that is praying."

"Praying!"

"Yes, Ray, praying. I'm going to say a prayer for you."

"Out here in the middle of the pond with no clothes on and you want to pray for me?"

"I can't think of a better time or place," Bonnie said soothingly.

Ray Wells, site supervisor for Big Burn Funeral Services, at that very moment, was shaken to his core. "Nobody prays for me," he said meekly.

"No one ever, Ray? That makes me sad."

The flirting tone was gone. Bonnie was talking earnestly. And Ray was realizing while he was treading water in the nude, mere feet away from a beautiful woman who was also treading water in the nude, that having somebody praying to God on your behalf was humbling — whether you were naked or not.

"Well, Aunt Nancy did for a little bit," Ray said quietly, "But then she kind of stopped."

"That's Tom's mom?"

"Yeah, she took me in after my folks had their accident."

"Tom told me about that."

"Aunt Nancy was good to me, and she prayed for me for a while, but then she stopped. I guess I kind of wore out her patience."

"I heard about that, too, Wrong Way Ray."

Ray, treading water, was looking deep into Bonnie's eyes. They were bright and sparkling and unspeakably green.

"But you do your God talking," added Bonnie.

"Big Tom told you that, too, didn't he?"

"Yes, he did," said Bonnie.

"Damn. That man just gave me away, didn't he?"

"Yes, he did," said Bonnie.

"Yes, I do God talking… every once in a while… when I really, I don't know, feel like I need to. I got that from Aunt Nancy."

"That's good, Ray," cooed Bonnie. "That's good. And here's me praying, Dear God, hear my prayer for this man, Ray Wells, to grow wiser, stronger, and more loving than he already is, in Your Name, amen."

Bonnie Betts gazed into his eyes as she spoke, and Ray Wells felt her words deep inside. Every single one. Never before had anyone prayed to God for him like that, right to his face, and never before had he ever felt like that. He was still Ray Wells swimming in the pond, but suddenly he was even bigger and broader. And it wasn't just him. The whole world felt different — ancient and reassuring and modern and exciting all at the same time. Ray Wells felt like at that moment he was part of the pond itself — quieted, cleansed, at peace, and smack dab in the circle of life. All thanks to Bonnie Betts and her prayers to God on his behalf. And as he floated in the water there in the gathering dusk, he sensed this beautiful angel woman had risen way up above him, as though she was speaking to him from a great height, showering him with her wisdom, and it came down upon him word by word, like raindrops dappling across the surface of his soul.

Eighteen

"No sex for forty days and forty nights, and you said yes?"

"I did. I absolutely did. I didn't know what else to do. She was praying for me. She was looking right at me all smiling and pretty and praying for me right in the middle of skinny dipping."

"Whoa, that ain't fair."

"No, it ain't fair. It's totally against the rules. You don't say yes to skinny dipping and then sit there and pray for me to be loving and wise. Hell, that just ruins the whole thing."

"Damn, she has got you tied up in knots," laughed Big Tom. "I knew I liked her."

Big Tom put his truck in park, and he and Ray hopped out. They were on the farm's southeastern corner, on a grassy swale overlooking three thousand Christmas trees — white pines, Douglas firs, Fraser firs. The harvest was six weeks out.

"So this is the plan," explained Big Tom. "We're going to pull these and put in campground number two. Trees go out the week before Thanksgiving. Then the work starts on campground two."

"Trees out, campground in, got it," said Ray. Then surveying the acreage spreading out before him, he said, "We're going to need some help."

"Yes, we are going to need some help," agreed Big Tom. "I'll tell Ken, then we can start looking for someone. Now that summer is over, guest bookings are slowing down, but we'll be busy with the build-out all the way through till spring."

Big Tom gestured toward a grove of hardwoods divided by a sizable stream. "Ken wants to put the trailer pads over there. Then campground here, and we'll build the number two pavilion and cooker site up the driveway toward the pine grove."

Ray nodded.

"Oh, and it's all going to be winterized, so, in the future we can do family funeral weekends even in cold weather."

"How does that work?" asked Ray.

"The final viewings and burns are outside, and everything else is inside. Big windows in the pavilion. It's kind of like an indoor-outdoor cremation. And he's going to set the campground up with rental trailers. Don't need no tents."

"No tents?"

"No tents unless they want to do winter camping, which most folks ain't doing."

"Smaller groups?" asked Ray.

"Smaller groups, bigger dollars. They got to rent the trailers for the overnight, but even then it's still a lot less than what they'd pay a funeral home. People die in the winter. Death don't wait for good weather. Families got to say final goodbyes in the winter. This way they can come out here and do it with us."

"That will be good," agreed Ray. "Less work, more money."

"Yeah, let's go look at the pavilion site," said Big Tom.

Ray followed him back into his pickup, thinking all the while about Bonnie. "You sure told her enough about me," he declared as he climbed in.

"Well, she was asking, so I just told the truth. Besides, Kelly was sitting there, so I had to tell it straight. Otherwise there would have been hell to pay."

"She was asking about me?"

"She was."

"When?"

"Like right from when she started staying with us, before me and Ken went to Florida."

"Huh."

"Yup, she's into you, dude."

"Huh."

"See, telling her the truth about you was the right thing to do."

"She's testing me. Definitely doing that."

"This looks about right," said Big Tom, pulling the truck off the driveway at the peak of a small hill. "Pavilion number two over there, cooker and viewing bier over there," he said, gesturing, with the motor running.

Ray nodded. Big Tom gave him a sideways glance and saw that Ray was deep in thought about Bonnie Betts. Shaking his head, he said, "And oh, by the way, Ken is very protective of her. He talked about her a lot when we were in Florida."

"He did?"

"Yeah, a lot."

"He told me not to mess with her right before you guys went to Florida," admitted Ray.

"Uh-oh, I didn't know that part of it."

"He told me not get stirred up with her, and here I am all stirred up with her."

"Uh-oh."

"Uh-oh is right. Thirty days left, and I'm about to burst. I mean, I'm on fire. There's no other way to say it. I am burning up for that girl. I'm jumping in the pond four times a day. And that ain't easy. That water is getting cold."

Big Tom was laughing. "She has got you right where she wants you."

"Hell is where she has me. I'm in hell and heaven at the same time. Heaven when I'm with her and she's smiling at me, hell, because that's all she lets me do. Smile and talk."

"And pray," laughed Big Tom.

"And pray," Ray exclaimed. "Yeah, we do that. We got a church date tomorrow."

"Church date? She's got you going to church?"

"Yeah, with you and Kelly."

"Wait, we're going to church tomorrow, all of us?"

"We're coming with you, and you ain't getting out of that."

"Oh, damn."

"Yep, damn."

And with that, Big Tom spun the wheel, gunned the engine, and headed the truck back to the farmhouse.

Nineteen

"I was proud of you putting that money in the collection basket, Ray," said Bonnie.

"I never done that before, but it felt good."

"The deacon sure was appreciative."

"Well, you give someone a couple twenties, they generally are," said Ray. "But, yeah, they seem like good people in that church. They were friendly."

"Thanks to Kelly and Tom talking us up."

"Yeah, thanks to Kelly and Tom. And may I say I truly enjoyed sitting next to you, as pretty as you are."

"Thank you, Ray," said Bonnie. "And I appreciate that you put on your Sunday best. You are quite handsome in that suit and tie. You look like the kind of man a girl can be proud to sit next to in church. But let's not forget that church is not about the beautiful clothes on your body, it's about the invisible beauty of your soul."

"Hah, invisible beauty," said Ray. "Honey, I can be sharp-dressed… generous… and blessed all at the same time, especially if I'm there with you."

Bonnie grinned and gave Ray's hand a squeeze. They were walking side-by-side on the trail along the Keeney Family Farm swim pond. Bonnie had agreed to let him fix her a cup of herb tea and show her his hunting bow. At first she had been hesitant, but Ray's church offering gave her just that extra little bit of persuasion to say okay.

Ray had parked his truck by the campground beach, and they were strolling along the path to Ray's yurt. It was a warm Sunday afternoon in the Shenandoahs. The early October leaves were just then revealing their fall colors, with the trees on mountaintops leading the way. Exhilaration was in the air.

"Uh-oh," gasped Ray, as he clutched at his leg.

"What? What's uh-oh?"

"I got ticks crawling on my leg," Ray said with apparent alarm. "I got to get them off. Fast. I ain't getting no Lyme disease." Ray dropped Bonnie's hand and slapped and swatted at his suit pants on his lower legs.

"What ticks? What Lyme disease?"

"Lyme disease. You get it from ticks. Little bugs crawl up on you and suck your blood. They live in the grass out here. You got any on you?"

"I don't know."

"Well, hurry, come on. We got to get to dock."

"Why?"

"It's safe there, no grass."

Bonnie was hurrying worriedly behind Ray who was fast walking up the path toward his swim dock. "Lyme disease, is it bad?" she asked, as she scanned the grass with alarm. "I never heard of it. We don't have it out in Vegas."

"I know," said Ray. "It's an Eastern thing. It's bad around here with these deer ticks. Lyme disease can really mess you up, saps your energy, makes your joints hurt, like an old lady, seriously bad disease," Ray said as he slapped and swatted at his pants, now up by his thigh. "Come on, hurry. Don't let them bite you."

"I don't feel like I'm getting bit."

"They're little and sneaky, almost invisible. And they're all in this long grass."

Ray made it to the dock with Bonnie close behind. He strode right over to the water's edge, kicked off his dress shoes, peeled off his socks, and dropped his trousers. Bonnie watched incredulously as he whipped off his suit coat, tie, shirt, undershirt, and finally his boxers, all the while making a big show of slapping at his legs with an alarming chorus of "oh, no's." Then finally, standing before her, fully nude and proud of himself, he gave Bonnie a cheeky grin and jumped in the pond.

"Come on in, the water's great," he said as he surfaced. "Wash those ticks right off you."

Bonnie Betts stood there at the edge of the swim dock, in her best Sunday dress. Tap, tap, tap went her stylish leather shoe on the dock's sun bleached wooden planks. She had her hands on her hips and was glaring at Ray Wells. "Ray Wells, do you think I am that silly of a girl to fall for this stunt?" she asked.

"Ain't no stunt," said Ray. "It's a tick check. Got to keep you from getting bit. It's for your health."

"Oh, really, for my health?"

"Yeah, best way forward is you slide out of that dress and come on in and wash those ticks off. Then I got to, you know, check you over to make sure they're all gone."

"Check me over."

"Head to toe, real close. Those critters are microscopic."

"Head to toe, is that it, Ray?"

"Every nook and cranny," said Ray. "Especially in your furry area. That's where they like to go."

"My furry area, Ray?"

"Yeah, your bikini place. Because those microscopic critters are, you know, microscopic."

Bonnie's foot tapping stopped abruptly as Ray, thrashing violently in the water, shouted, "Oh, ouch, oh, the freshwater dolphins are biting them ticks right off my body, oh, ouch." Then he stopped thrashing and smiled wickedly. "Oh, oh," he purred. "That is so sexy. Keep going, you freshwater dolphins. Keep biting. Keep nibbling."

Bonnie Bells began grinning like a girl who had just bought her first new car. "Ray Wells, are you suggesting I am supposed to undress myself here on this beautiful Sunday afternoon," she asked in mock incredulity, "jump in the water to join you for a skinny dip, and then submit to you rummaging around my body for microscopic critters that congregate in my..."

"Furry places," repeated Ray.

"Furry places," echoed Bonnie. "And I assume that means I have to stay naked for this examination?"

"Head to toe," said Ray. "Until I'm positive there are no ticks anywhere on your person."

"Ray, it sounds to me like you've done this before."

"I have," he said. "I'm very experienced and very professional. Ticks do not like me because I always get what I'm after."

"Well, in that case, if you're professional about it," Bonnie cooed, as she unzipped the back of her dress.

###

"This is nice," sighed Ray.

"It sure is," agreed Bonnie. "Thank you for my tick check. You were very thorough. And I appreciate that you kept your hands to yourself, as I asked."

"Demanded is more like it," grumbled Ray.

They were fully nude, lying side by side on the dock. No towels. No chairs. Just them, laying face up on the wooden planks, soaking up the Indian summer sunshine.

"That was not easy," said Ray.

"I could tell. You keep jumping in the pond."

"Closest thing I got to a cold shower," he said. "And I need about ten of those right now."

Bonnie giggled. "You and your tick check."

"Can't we just take a timeout on this forty-day thing and roll around a little bit? Just, you know, piggyback on over to my fur pile."

"Nope, not doing it."

"Come on, just a little make-out session. You can tie my hands behind my back."

Bonnie, who had been staring up into the clouds, tilted her head and gave Ray a sideways glance. "Dear God in Heaven," she prayed, "please help Ray Wells understand that he's got twenty-nine more days to wait before he has any kind of a make-out session with me. Amen."

Ray snorted, "Huh."

Bonnie, raising her eyebrows at Ray, continued, "And, God, please also help Ray understand that when we do finally have that make-out session, it will be everything he'd hoped for and more. But he has to wait."

"Damn," exclaimed Ray. And he stood up and jumped straight into the pond.

Later, after he'd swum for a few minutes, he climbed back to stand beside Bonnie, dripping wet, head to toe. "How come you pray to God when you pray for me? I thought you were a Jesus girl. How come you don't pray to Jesus for me?"

Bonnie smiled broadly, lifted herself up on an elbow, and struck a seductive pose. "Oh, Ray, honey," she murmured, in a kitten voice, "I'll pray to Jesus for you if you need me to, but I usually go straight up to God for you because I know you need the extra strength version."

Once again Ray Wells was staring deep into Bonnie Betts' intoxicating green eyes. She was laying out before him like the most beautiful naked lady painting in the history of art, and she was — again — praying for him. Ray Wells had always considered himself intelligent, but he had along the way left the whiz kid stuff to other folks — the algorithms, the theories, the coding. It wasn't that he wasn't smart, he just wasn't that kind of smart. But the one thing he was smart about was knowing how to keep Right Way Ray from falling back into being Wrong Way Ray. And right then and there, Right Way Ray knew what he had to do. And he turned and jumped straight into that pond.

When Ray returned to lie down beside Bonnie, she was stretched out on her belly, hands straight down by her side, eyes closed, a beautiful woman at peace in the sunshine. "It's Sunday afternoon, Ray, and you ain't over there with Tom watching the baseball playoff," she murmured contentedly.

"I know," he said, easing face-down into his spot beside her. "Being with you is a lot better."

"Especially since we're naked."

"Yeah, that's most of it," agreed Ray.

"You got to be careful of your pale parts, Ray," Bonnie murmured, as she lazily looked him over. "Don't get sunburned."

"You ain't got no tan lines," he observed.

"No, I do not," said Bonnie. "I spend a lot of time sunbathing like this and I take care not to get burned. I started doing it for my job, and now I just do it because I like it. It keeps me real. This is the birthday suit God gave me. He made me beautiful right out of my mother's womb and I want him to see I still am."

"Well, he did a hell of a job because I am a big fan of your birthday suit," said Ray.

Bonnie, eyes closed, sighed, and started another prayer: "Dear God …"

"What? What I do?" asked Ray.

"Please help us understand how to use better words than the ugly ones like hell and damn and shit and all the rest."

Ray sighed. "Okay, I could see that," he agreed. "I do talk a little rough."

"Yes, you do," said Bonnie. "I know what those words mean, but the less I hear them, the better I feel."

"Yeah, okay," agreed Ray. "I hear you. Tell me about this job you had where you didn't want no tan lines."

Bonnie sighed deeply. "I knew this time was coming," she said. "I prayed all through church for the strength to do it right."

What followed was a long and winding narration, which Ray listened to in rapt silence. Bonnie told about growing up in Vegas with a single mom who died of cancer her senior year of high school. She talked about how she had gone from being a popular cheerleader to the girl with no mom or dad. She talked about how Uncle Ken, who had come out every year on her birthday, came for her mom's funeral. She talked about how her mom's last request was for her and Uncle Ken to scatter her ashes in the desert together. That was three years ago, but then Uncle Ken had gotten so busy with this funeral business, he stopped checking in.

She talked about how she lied about her age for her job at The Garden, a strip club with murals of snakes and half-eaten apples on the walls. She talked about waitressing topless. "A thong and pasties on my nipples, and men just fell over for me." She talked about the girls she worked with, how they were used by the managers who got them pregnant and then forced them into abortions. "Lose the baby or lose the job," was the order.

She talked about being sexy in Vegas and sexy in The Garden and how she could no longer stand the word. "Sexy is all about money. Sexy is just so men can make money off of women. That's all it is," she said, shaking her head. "Sexy just means men are selling stuff and using a woman's body to do it. They sure used mine. I made a lot of money for those managers in The Garden, and I definitely got my cut, so, yes, I did it. I let myself be that way. I made that choice. It was hard not to. I made better money wiggling and jiggling than most college girls ever do. But it was the wrong choice because it was killing me inside, Ray. I could feel it. My mom was healthy and careful about everything. No drinking, no smoking, no drugs. She raised me so I don't do any of that. But it was all around me. I could feel it coming for me, and she wasn't there to help me. I had to get out. I had to. I remembered about Uncle Ken's farm way out in Virginia, and I got in my car and here I am."

"And you found Jesus in Des Moines."

"Yes, indeed, I found Jesus in Des Moines. That would never have happened if I hadn't left. God is guiding me. I really believe that."

Ray thought for a moment before replying. "Well, I'm glad you found Jesus," he said. "And I'm glad you left Vegas. And I don't think of you as sexy. Beautiful, yes. Maybe it's the praying you do for me. And with me. But, no, not sexy. Not you. Beautiful, yes. Sexy, no. Don't get me wrong I would do it with you at the drop of a hat. But it wouldn't be sexy, it would be beautiful."

"Ray Wells, thank you for telling me I'm not sexy."

"Uhm, you're welcome."

"And I think you're beautiful, too." And with that, Bonnie Betts kissed the tip of her pointer finger and leaned over and touched it to Ray Wells' lips. "But you've still got twenty-nine days."

Twenty

"Daddy is concerned about you, Bonnie."

Bonnie shot Kim a questioning glance. "Why is Uncle Ken concerned about me?" she asked.

"Because I told him you've been dating Ray Wells."

Kim was driving the Big Burn hearse, Bonnie was in the front passenger's seat. They were returning from a body drop-off. Bonnie had helped Ray stretcher the body, a hefty ex-baseball star, from the back of the hearse to the viewing bier, all while Kim watched them from the comfort of the front seat. They had left Ray there to light the pyre and manage the after-party.

"Oh, that?" exclaimed Bonnie, with a giggle. "He's got nothing to worry about. Ray is a gentleman."

"Ray Wells is a gentleman?" Kim asked sarcastically.

"Yes," replied Bonnie. "He took me out for dinner last night in Charlottesville, and we had a lovely evening."

"Where did he take you, Dairy Queen?"

Bonnie laughed. "No, he took me to the Italian Inn. We went with Kelly and Tom. It was really fun, and the food was great."

"Well, aren't you just fitting right into a fantastic foursome?"

"Yes, and you're welcome to join us, Kim."

Kim smiled ironically. "No thank you," she said in her corporate tone, "Ray and Tom are inseparable, and it's great that you and Kelly are now friends. But I have different social circles. We'll just leave it there."

Ignoring Kim's mean girl tone, Bonnie bubbled on: "We are all so excited for Kelly's baby. She and I have painted the walls creamy yellow, with white trim and butterfly murals. It's so cute. And Ray and Tom are being very supportive. I don't know if you know this, but I've got Ray going to church with me. I really like him. More and more every day. And please tell Uncle Ken to talk to me about it directly. We've got nothing to hide. Ray and I like each other, but we are proceeding with the help of Jesus."

Kim wrinkled her face in disgust. "What does that mean, with the help of Jesus?" she asked.

"It means, we are praying for each other. And it means we are not doing anything physically romantic for forty days or forty nights. Not even kissing. Just like when Jesus fasted in the desert to resist the devil, that's what we're doing. And believe me, it ain't easy with Ray Wells."

Kim pulled the hearse into its parking spot outside of the Metal Barn. She put it in park and shut off the engine, then she turned to face Bonnie. "Ray Wells has had dozens upon dozens of girls in that little hut of his," she stated, sounding like a judge reading out criminal charges. "Sometimes he has two different girls in the same week. How he's stayed disease-free and out of trouble with pregnancies for these two years is beyond me, but prayers ain't ever going to work for that guy, especially from someone like you."

"What's that supposed to mean?"

"Daddy told me about your 'job' at a strip club in Las Vegas. Then you come out here pretending to be a Jesus girl. Oh, surprise, surprise you find your way right to Ray Wells, the biggest slut in county. Birds of a feather. You can't run away from your past, Bonnie. Not here at Keeney Family Farm. We got a business to run, and having two sluts on the staff is not good for business. That's what that's supposed to mean."

A range of emotions flew across Bonnie's face — fury, anguish, determination. "Being in a relationship with your co-worker doesn't make you a slut," she said with lowered eyes. "Just look at Tom and Kelly."

"Tom and Kelly are married. They were married when Tom started here. Tom's not a slut like Ray."

Bonnie's eyes flashed to meet Kim's condescending stare. "Ray and I like each other, and we are taking it slow. There's nothing wrong with that."

"Birds of a feather," Kim repeated.

For a moment Bonnie gazed straight ahead, unwilling to even look in Kim's direction. Then she placed her hands palm-down on the dashboard, breathed in, and exhaled a deep cleansing breath, then she folded her hands. "Dear God," she prayed in a quavering voice, "please forgive Kim for her harsh and dishonest words directed at me and Ray. I know she had a hard childhood without her mother, as did Ray without either of his parents, as did I without a father. Please help Kim find the healing and love that Ray and I have found with each other, in the name of your son, Jesus Christ. Amen."

"Don't you dare pray for me," hissed Kim. "And don't you dare talk about my mother."

Bonnie turned with a steely look and said, "Kim, you keep your ugly comments and ugly thoughts about me and Ray to yourself, and I'll keep my prayers for you to myself. But I will not stop praying for you, mostly because I love you, but also because you need it. Now, if there's nothing else for today, I'll head over to Kelly and Tom's."

"Well, no, Bonnie, that's not all. This hearse needs a good cleaning — inside and out."

"Fine, I'll take it to the car wash."

"You do that," Kim said. And she jumped out of the hearse and stalked off, leaving Bonnie the keys and control of the hearse.

Twenty-One

"You found Kim's panties from the back of the Escalade?" Kelly was aghast at the sight of Bonnie holding aloft a pair of navy blue panties in a Ziplock plastic bag.

"Well, if they're not yours and they're not mine, they got to be hers."

"Oh, that is so gross," said Kelly with a shudder.

"Yeah, she had me take the Escalade to the car wash yesterday. I found them when I vacuumed out the back. They were all blended in with carpet back there. Plus there was an empty condom wrapper in the door well," added Bonnie.

Kelly shuddered, "Ewww."

"I think it was when she was with Anthony," continued Bonnie. "She's been moping around ever since he went back to Tasmania."

"Yeah, I think you're right on that. They were all over each other for a couple of weeks there."

"They sure were. She showed him all over — Skyline Drive, Charlottesville. They even went into D.C. for three days. All while Ken and Tom were down in Florida."

"Wow, she showed him the town."

"She showed him a lot more than the town," said Bonnie. "And she calls me slut."

"Bonnie, you got to be careful with her," cautioned Kelly. "She's the boss's daughter."

"I know. I know what she is. But I know what I am, and she has no right to say anything ugly about me or Ray."

"Are you going to give them back to her?"

Bonnie smiled broadly and said, "Yes, I am."

Twenty-Two

"Wow, great pizza, Bonnie," said Big Tom, as he cut himself a bite with his knife and fork.

"I love the crust," added Kelly.

"Damn, this is good," said Ray, who, as soon as the words had left his mouth, and he saw Bonnie raising her eyebrows at him, issued a correction. "I mean holy wow, this is good."

Bonnie sighed and nodded. "Thank you, Ray, for your thoughtful compliment."

"This is like the pizza at the restaurant in Vegas where your mom always took me," said Ken.

Bonnie nodded. "Yeah, my friend Lizzie's family runs that restaurant. They're Sicilian. They taught me how to cook all kinds of good stuff. We went out to the Italian Inn the other night, and I just wanted to trot out my Sicilian dishes. There will be more."

"Awesome," said Big Tom, with Kelly nodding along.

"Can't wait," said Ken.

Kim nibbled a slice but then set it aside, commenting, "It's a little too crusty for me," which prompted an exchange of glances between Kelly and Bonnie.

"Kimmy, you're missing out," Ken said as he held his slice aloft and examined it. "This is good pizza. And it's original. It's not like crappy delivery pizza. We should serve this at our campground lunches."

"Oh, there's an idea," echoed Big Tom. "I think this would be a big hit. What do you think, Kel?"

"Definitely," agreed Kelly.

Kim, surprised by her dad's zeal, quickly added, "The kids would love it. But would Bev and Myrna make it? Or does Bonnie? I mean, who makes it, transports it, et cetera?"

Bonnie looked up from the baking sheet, as she dished Ray up a second slice. "Bev and Myrna can make it. I can show them how. They'd probably love it. I cooked some zucchini soup for them when I was there, they loved that. They could do this easy."

"Yes, yes, and yes," said Ken. "Bonnie, get in touch with Bev and Myrna and tell them about your Sicilian pizza. Tell them we think it could be a campground lunch. Let's do a group tasting with them."

"Okay," said Bonnie. "But let me ask you, on a scale of one to ten, you see that as a …"

"Ten," said Ken, without hesitation. "Make it happen. Next week."

"Okay, I will," said Bonnie.

"And that soup sounds good," said Ray. "Can I suggest we have some at our next meeting?"

"Yes, Ray," Bonnie said sweetly. "You can suggest that we have zucchini soup at our next meeting. And I'd be happy to help you cook it. I'll coach and you cook. And by the way, you'll be doing the dishes when it's over."

Ray nodded helplessly as Big Tom, Kelly, and Ken all chuckled.

"So, let's get to it," said Ken. "Burns are slowing down a bit with cold weather coming in."

"Alternative funeral services, Daddy," corrected Kim.

"Alternative funeral services," echoed Ken, "are slowing down with cold weather coming in. But we got a lot on our agenda. First, we harvest the trees from the southeast parcel, then the build-out for campground number two. And we're going to need help for all that. Rather than put an ad in the paper, I reached out through our contacts and I think I found a good hire. Bev's nephew has dropped out of high school and is now living with her. I met him. He's a good kid, good family. He needs the work, we need the help, so I hired him. Deandre will start tomorrow morning."

"Deandre?" asked Big Tom.

"Yes, Deandre Pounds. He goes by D."

"D?" asked Ray.

"Yeah, D," said Ken. "Mom is a detective in the Petersburg Police Department, just south of Richmond. And dad is a sergeant major, runs the transportation units out of Fort Lee."

"Sergeant major, those dudes don't play," said Big Tom.

"No, they don't," agreed Ken. "But D has apparently got himself tied in with a bad crowd, bad enough for them to get him out of town. He comes here, lives with Bev, works with us, learns some skills, makes some bucks. We get the help we need. It's a win-win."

"Okay, D comes on tomorrow, and we start setting up the harvest?" asked Ray.

"Yep, we got three thousand trees this year. Trucks come week before Thanksgiving," said Tom.

"Then we start on campground two," added Ray.

"Sounds good," said Ken. "It's going to be a lot of work around here, but it's going to pay off big time when we have both campgrounds full."

"Big work, big pay," said Big Tom to a general chorus of "oh, yeahs."

"On that note, though," Kim interjected. "I've been invited to go to Tasmania to spend Christmas and New Year's with Anthony and his family."

A stunned silence settled over the group.

"Christmas and New Year's," Ken asked, finally.

"Yes, I just made my flight reservations," said Kim. "I leave Friday after Thanksgiving and come back the end of January."

"End of January, for real?" asked Ray.

"Yeah, that's right."

"That's two months," said Ken. "Two very important months, and you'll be leaving us high and dry."

"I know it's a long time, Daddy," said Kim, in a little girl sing-song. "But I've wanted to do this, like, forever. Winters here are so dreary. I'd be down there for their summer, and I'll be with Anthony. I don't know where this will lead for me and him, but I have to see. I've already made the reservations. They can't be changed."

No one spoke. But all eyes were fixed questioningly on Kim. And it was just then that Bonnie went to a brown paper bag she had on the kitchen counter next to her purse, and said, "Oh, hey, Kim, I found these in the hearse the other day. I think they're yours. Kelly said they're not hers. They're certainly not mine. And you're the only person driving the hearse, so here you go." And Bonnie walked over to Kim with the brown paper bag, pulled out the plastic bag that contained the lacy, navy blue panties, and laid them on the table next to Kim, knowing that everyone in the room could see it.

"Those aren't mine," Kim said flatly without even looking at the bag.

"These panties aren't yours?" Bonnie asked incredulously.

"Never seen them, not mine. Are they yours?"

"Nope," said Bonnie, "too big for me or Kelly. And since I found them in the Escalade, you know, when you asked me to clean it out the other day, I figured they were yours."

"Well, you figured wrong," said Kim.

"Let me see that," said Ken. Bonnie handed him the bag. "This looks like stuff I see in our laundry, Kim," he said flatly. "These aren't yours?"

"No."

"Were you out in the Escalade with that Anthony guy?" asked Ken.

"No, Daddy, I was not," Kim said with a flurry of eye blinks.

Ken put a big hand on the side of his face and rubbed and rubbed — rubbed his cheek, rubbed his eyes, rubbed his forehead. No one spoke. Finally he fixed his gaze on his daughter and said, "Okay, Kimmy, you got your two months in Tasmania with this man."

All eyes turned to Kim, who smirked her delight.

"We," Ken paused, "well, mostly I will pick up your slack. But we do not appreciate having to do it at such an important time. Now, I can see this is important for you. And since we're basically a family here, we're going to support you. Right, everyone?"

Heads nodded.

"That said," he continued, "this business is shared by everyone in this room. It's not your toy to play with, Kim. It's no one's toy to play with. Everyone in this room can prosper by growing this business big as it can get, and that's what we're going to do. Grow and prosper. Between now and Thanksgiving, these next six weeks, I want you to show Bonnie and Kelly how you do your job. Just the basics, but you got to show them how to do bookings, body pickups, death certificate registrations, all that. We are all going to learn what all the jobs are, so we can fill in. It's going to be busy, busy, busy, and we're going to be training people to help us. Big Tom and Ray have a very busy couple of months ahead, and that includes having a baby, right, Kelly?"

"That is right," said Kelly.

"So, Kim, you want to take a two-month vacation halfway around the world, you got to share your responsibilities," said Ken.

"But, Daddy," Kim protested, frowning.

"No buts," said Ken.

"Does that mean Kim has to learn prep and shroud?" asked Bonnie. "Because she never has. Everybody has but her."

"No way, I'm not doing that," said Kim.

"Yes," said Ken, "I agree with Bonnie. I think you need to understand that job, too. If we're a family supporting you, you can do your share. If that means learning prep and shroud, then, yes, you do."

Bonnie beamed. Kim glared. Big Tom, Kelly, and Ray grinned in unison.

"And let me just say," said Ken, "about relationships. Bonnie, to me, you are a young girl. I know that's not how you see yourself, but that's how I see you. And I say that as someone who watched you grow up from the day you were born. I know that you and Ray are dating. I appreciate that you are taking it slow and following the path of Jesus. I really do. And you have my approval to keep on path together. Slowly on that path."

At that, Kim straightened on her kitchen stool and asked breathlessly, with a shocked look on her face: "Wait, you were there when she was born, in Las Vegas?"

"Yes, Kim," Ken said evenly, "I was there when Bonnie was born because… well, I'm her daddy."

"I KNEW IT," shouted Bonnie. "I KNEW YOU WERE MY DADDY!" And she flung herself into Ken's arms for the first father-daughter hug they had ever had on the Keeney Family Farm.

And as he held his youngest daughter close, murmuring over and over, "Welcome home, honey, welcome home," he watched as his eldest daughter slid from her seat and fell unconscious to his kitchen floor.

Twenty-Three

"What do you think, D?" asked Ray. "It ain't that bad out here."

"No, man, it ain't bad," replied Deandre.

Big Tom was driving Ken's rusty, rattly Chevy pickup. Hand-crank windows cracked to breeze away the old pickup smell. It was a two-door with a bench seat. Deandre was in the middle. Ray was on the window seat. They were three dirty, sweaty men who didn't care about the decades of mud ground into the floor or the decades of dust ground into the seats. They were done for the day. "Long days," added Big Tom.

"Long days is right," agreed Deandre.

"But what else you going to do out here?" asked Ray.

"Ain't much else to do," agreed Deandre.

"D, you know how to drive a stick?" asked Ray, as Tom shifted from first to second gear.

"No, ain't never done that."

"Well, we'll get you learned up on that."

"All right," said D. "Going to drive like Fast and Furious dudes."

"Well, maybe eventually," said Ray. "Ain't hard, just got to learn it."

"But you had that chainsaw working real good at the end," added Big Tom.

"Yeah, man, I ain't never use a chainsaw before," Deandre said, grinning.

"Yeah, you had that going like a pro," said Ray.

"You picked that up fast, man. First shot at being a redneck, and you come through with flying colors," Big Tom chuckled.

"Ricky Bobby," laughed Deandre.

"Ha."

"That movie is funny as hell," said Ray.

"I seen it with my dad," agreed Deandre. "Them dudes are funny."

"Yeah, so tomorrow we got a lot more clearing to do beside that stream," said Big Tom. "All those hardwoods coming out for the new campground. Then we got some bush hogging to do around the Christmas trees to clear out the weeds for the harvest. So, more chainsawing, and you'll learn to drive to the tractor and the mower. We call that bush hogging."

"Chainsawing and bush hogging, damn, if Mama could see me now."

"Ha."

"And then we got a burn coming up day after tomorrow," said Ray. "So you'll work with me on that and learn that. It ain't complicated what we do out here, but we make good money. That job mostly is attitude. You just got to be there for those families in their tough time."

"I know that. Aunt Bev loves what you guys do. She filled me in."

"Bev and Myrna been doing real well with us," said Ray.

"Yeah, they doing it," said Deandre.

"Yeah, they are," echoed Big Tom. "Bev and Myrna put a lot of love in their cooking."

"We get so many compliments on the food in the after-parties," agreed Ray. "But, hey, D, I got to tell you this, man straight up," Ray added in a suddenly serious tone, as both Big Tom and Deandre looked over. "When I came out here I wasn't much different than you," said Ray. "Wrong Way Ray is what they called me. I was all street and down with it. And then Tom pulled me in and said, work with me. My first month out here I was just going around looking for places to plant weed because I was going to sell me some weed off this farm."

"You were?" asked Big Tom, surprised.

"Yeah, I was," said Ray, "Straight up. But I realized that was dumb."

"I ain't looking to sell no weed," said Deandre.

"I didn't say you were. I said you're like I was, thinking you're still in the streets."

"Because that's what Aunt Bev told us, the back story. She loves you like she loves us. So she filled us in too," said Big Tom.

"She did?"

"Yeah, she did," said Ray. "So just understand, the only thing we'll be selling off this farm down in Richmond is Christmas trees. You feel me?"

"I feel you, man."

"Not saying you're doing nothing, D, just saying what if."

"I feel you, man."

"We put people on the team, we want them to stay on the team, and then we all make money. Good team, good money. Just ask Bev," said Big Tom.

"Yeah, I know, man, I know."

"So you feel me on all that?" asked Ray.

"Good team, good money — I feel you, man," Deandre replied.

"All right," said Big Tom. "Hey, so, D, why don't you come on over tonight. Bonnie is cooking her awesome Sicilian pizza. We're watching World Series Game Six. And Ray is doing everything Bonnie tells him to do, including the dishes, which is almost more entertaining than the baseball game."

Deandre started laughing. "Definitely coming to see that."

"You guys laugh now," said Ray. "But Bonnie and I are taking a half day together on Friday because that's our big day."

"That's your big day, Friday, Halloween?"

"Yeah, forty days and forty nights is over Friday, when I wake up. I didn't even realize until last week when she told me to make big plans for our "special" Halloween. So I'll come out in the morning, work half day, then we're going into Charlottesville. I got a fancy room with a big surprise. We got some costumes. We're going out, walking around in our costumes with all the U.VA kids."

"What kind of surprise," asked Big Tom.

"Romantic surprise," said Ray, grinning.

Tom and Deandre chuckled like they were proud of Ray, which they were.

"Hell, you'll fit right in with those U.VA kids," said Big Tom. "She's younger than half of them. They'll be looking at you, dude, like what is he doing with her."

"Well, they'll definitely be looking at her."

"Uh-oh, what's her costume?"

"I ain't saying."

"What's your costume?"

"I ain't saying that, either."

"It's some kind Jesus girl thing, though, right?"

"I ain't saying on that. All I'm saying is they will definitely be looking at her."

"So you've seen her costume?"

"Oh, yeah. She's been teasing me with it for a week."

"Uh-oh."

"Uh-oh is right."

Twenty-Four

"Ghosts all over this town, not just on Halloween. Every time I see this statue I think of all these damn Charlottesville ghosts."

"Ray…"

"No, I'm serious this time. Damned is what they are, and it ain't their doing. They got led into it."

It was afternoon. Ray and Bonnie, still in their work clothes, had finished their late lunch and were dawdling through Charlottesville while the inn was getting their room ready.

"Ray, that's just an old statue of a guy on a horse. We're the only ones here. Doesn't look to me like anybody even cares about it. Why let it upset you? "

"It's history, honey. Southern history. That's General Robert E. Lee. Not sure why they got him up here in Charlottesville. Appomattox is just down the road."

"What's Appomattox?"

"It's town where he surrendered to the Yankees. They got a whole Civil War thing there, too."

"A lot of history around here. We don't have that in Vegas… well, except for mob history. But that's not that old."

"Yeah, we got it around here. bloody Southern history. But more than that, my history is tied up with that man, too. The Wells Family used to own part of Ken's farm."

Bonnie eyes grew big as she watched Ray. He was staring up at that statue like it held a lie that only he could see.

"Yeah, the Wells Family owned the part of the farm where we're working now. They had the parcel of land along that stream, where we're putting in campground number two, all the way up into the pine grove."

"Wow, I did not know that."

"Yeah, Big Tom and I talk about it every once in a while. Right up in that pine grove. Old stone walls are still there."

"That's the prettiest part of the farm."

"I think so. But anyway, the Wells boys fought and died under that man right there. My great grandfather's grandfather was born on that farm. His daddy and his uncle went to war and didn't come back. General Robert E. Lee walked away from Appomattox, they didn't even get there."

Ray gestured to the statue. "Family was lost without their men, carpetbagger bought them off the land, sold it, eventually, to the Keeneys. They've had it ever since, and the Wells never really got over it."

"Does Ken know this?"

"I don't think he does, actually. I've never talked about it with Ken."

"Okay, but you're talking about it with his daughter, so if he doesn't already know, he's going to find out."

Now it was Ray's turn for his eyes to grow wide. "But really, it ain't all that big a deal," he said quickly. "It's old family history. It doesn't involve us now. People spend too much time reaching back into old stuff, they just mess themselves up. You got to live your present. That's what Big Tom taught me. It's what he teaches me every day. It ain't easy for him to put that leg on and shrug off his war wounds."

"Well, I got some old stuff I got to settle with Ken."

"Yeah, I guess you do."

They stood there a while looking up at the statue as the afternoon shadows lengthened. "You got a plan on that?"

No plan, just praying and trusting the Lord."

"Damn — I mean, darn, I love when you say that."

Bonnie smiled and took Ray's hand. "Dear God," she prayed, "please help Ray Wells understand how much I love him. Amen."

Ray Wells cradled Bonnie's face in his hands for a long, deep kiss. "I love you, Bonnie Betts," he whispered.

"I love you, Ray Wells," she whispered back.

"Feels good to be able to kiss you finally," he said, after.

"You definitely earned that kiss."

"Forty days and forty nights for just one kiss?"

"Well, forty days and forty nights for a maybe yes, maybe no, depending on how I feel about it. That time was a yes.”

“I can live with that,” Ray chuckled. “Come on, let’s go see what’s going on with that room. I got a surprise waiting for you.”

# # #

“Now I see why you put us in this musty old inn,” said Bonnie.

“Yep, isn’t that cool?”

“It’s like really cool.”

Ray and Bonnie, overnight bags in hand, were peeking into the bathroom of their suite in one of Charlottesville’s grand old inns, marveling at its hundred-year-old clawfoot tub. Behind them was a queen bed, all nicely made up. Antique lithographs of fox hunters hung on the walls. The moment they walked in the room, they felt special, like they were going back in history, leaving their everyday lives behind for a time travel adventure.

“Why, it’s big enough for both of us.”

“Darn, right,” said Ray with a self-congratulatory smile. “And the faucets are in the middle, so we can sit back comfortably at both ends and… talk.”

“Oooh, sudsy bathtub talk?” asked Bonnie.

“Warm, sudsy bathtub talk,” agreed Ray. “We ain’t doing no cold water skinny dipping today.”

Bonnie giggled. “No we are not,” she said. And, dropping her bag, she went over and turned on the faucets. Water blasted out, bubbles foamed when she added the herbal scented bubble bath. “Perfect,” she said as she tested the water and wetted the loofah.

Ray dropped his bag where he stood. First things first, unpacking could wait. "Are you just going to stand there watching?" she asked, finally.

"Yep," said Ray. "If I waited forty days and forty nights, I can take my time and ease into this."

"Oh, is that so?" asked Bonnie, unbuttoning her blouse.

"Yes, that's so," said Ray, who was standing straight—backed with his arms crossed.

Bonnie, humming to herself, hung her blouse on the clothes rack, then unbuttoned her jeans and hung them so they wouldn't get wrinkled. After her socks and shoes, she slipped off her bras, with a wink for Ray. "Remember these?" she cooed.

"How could I forget," smiled Ray Wells.

Bonnie Betts smirked, slipped off her underwear, and disappeared up to her chin into the bubbles. "Oh, Ray," she exclaimed, "this is luxurious. You are such a good man for thinking this up for us."

Ray nodded in agreement. "I feel like a good man," he said. But he made no move to undress.

"Oh my, oh my," squealed Bonnie. "I do believe there are freshwater dolphins in this tub. Oh, they are playful. Now how did they get in here?"

Ray smiled, but stood still with his arms crossed.

Bonnie splashed and sponged. Finally she asked, "Are you coming in here? Why you holding back?"

"Well, I mean, I been thinking about this for forty days and forty nights, and I know you have, too.”

“Yes, that’s right, honey, I have — maybe not with the same devotion as you, but I have.”

“Well, I’m just thinking what if… like what if it’s not up to expectations, what if you’re disappointed?”

“Oh, sweetheart, is that what it is?” Bonnie giggled and lifted her tan and toned leg out of the bath, pointing her red painted toes at the ceiling with the grace of a gymnast. “Ray, honey, I think you should know I’m in my lull.”

“Your what?”

“My fertility lull. In others words, we can do it for a few days without using a rubber, and I still won’t get pregnant.”

“For real?”

“Yes, honey, it’s the rhythm method, no condoms necessary.”

“Damn — I mean, darn,” gushed Ray.

Bonnie Betts laid her arms along the side of the tub and giggled delightedly as over the next five seconds Ray Wells flung his clothes into every corner of the bathroom and launched himself into that tub with a sudsy splash.

# # #

Halloween evening was warm that year. The skies were clear and starry when Ray and Bonnie left their room. They almost didn’t want to go out, so pleasant was it to lay there naked in each other’s arms. But life was waiting, and so they roused themselves, put on their costumes, and went to see what it held in store for them.

Hand in hand down Main Street they walked, Ray costumed in his high school baseball uniform, bat over his shoulder, mitt stuck on the end of the bat, cap tilted back on his head, cleats clattering on the sidewalk. Bonnie, his personal cheerleader, wore her uniform she'd kept from high school, complete with red jump panties and red training shoes to match her red and white dress.

The other costumed revelers on Main Street were headed toward the U.VA campus just like Ray and Bonnie. One large group of what looked like frat brothers were dressed as Dalmatian puppies. Red plastic cups in hand, they wagged and woofed their way toward the Green, the storied heart of the campus, and the throbbing center of Charlottesville's Halloween celebration.

Thousands were milling about the Green when Ray and Bonnie arrived. Monsters were everywhere, devils, too. Undergrad girls were costumed as saucy wenches, undergrad boys as superheroes. Families were there for the excitement. Children paraded as the cartoon characters they adored. Pirates and wizards were popular with the grad students. Of course, the Star Wars properties were well represented, as were scarecrows and Dorothys, witches and vampires. It was Virginia, so there were warriors — from Roman centurions to OIF grunts. A group of gray-coated Rebs stood in a cluster off by themselves, replica rifles at the ready. And, yes, there were fairies, scantily clad boys and girls in glittery makeup, posing happily for any phone that recorded their antics.

"Wow," said Ray, "I always wanted to see this. Kids in high school would come down here and rave about it. This is huge."

Bonnie scanned the gathering, nodding politely. "Ray, honey," she said, "I grew up in Vegas. I've been doing Halloween on the Strip since I was a little kid. This is fun, but it ain't huge."

Ray chuckled. "I always wanted to do this on Halloween," he said, taking Bonnie by her hand, "just go right in the middle of the biggest party, with the prettiest girl there, and give her a trick or treat."

And so Ray Wells, site manager for Big Burn Funeral Services, laid his bat and glove down on the ground. He took Bonnie Betts, assistant to the director for Big Burn Funeral Services, into his arms and whispered, "Trick or treat," and kissed her with a full forty days of desire.

# # #

Later, in the soundless dark of their hotel suite, as they lay in each other's arms, feeling more than seeing, talking contentedly with each other in the languorous way of young lovers. "So how many more days can we do this, you know, without the rubber?" murmured Ray.

"A couple, but the more you do it, the riskier it gets," whispered Bonnie.

"So if you got pregnant what would you do?" asked Ray, growing more alert.

"Ray Wells, if I get pregnant, it will be our baby," Bonnie replied firmly. "And we will raise that baby, plus all his or her brothers and sisters, as our family."

"Our family?"

"Our family. There is no doubt in my mind my future is with you. You will be the father of all my children."

"So you and me having a family?" asked Ray, now fully alert.

"A big, beautiful family," answered Bonnie.

"I take it we're getting married."

"Dear God, thank you for hearing my prayers to help this man, Ray Wells, be stronger, wiser, and more loving … but especially wiser on account of him listening to my gentle feminine persuasions. Amen."

Ray laughed. "So I guess we're going ring shopping."

"Yes, we are."

Ray sighed. "Sounds good to me," he said. "By the way, how many babies you talking about in this big, beautiful family of ours?"

"Oh, I don't know, ten or fifteen."

"FIFTEEN!" Ray Wells sat bolt upright in the inky dark as though he'd backed into an electric fence.

"Oh, sweetheart," cooed Bonnie sleepily, as she found his back and gave him a reassuring rub, "trick or treat."

Twenty-Five

"We're out here in the middle of Madison County, standing on dry land, trimming trees, and you look seasick," laughed Big Tom.

"A dozen babies," sighed Ray, as he lopped the bottom layer of branches off a Fraser fir. "She's talking like we're going to have a dozen babies."

"Well, God, has a say in it too, though, doesn't he?" asked Big Tom.

"Oh, yeah, and I keep pointing that out," Ray replied, crouching low for a big branch. "But she's going on and on about having a baby in her arms for the next twenty years."

Deandre, who was working the row of trees beside Ray, stood up, gave him a sympathetic look, and uttered a long, low, "Damn."

"Yeah," said Ray, "a dozen years of babies, which means that's another twenty years before the youngest is up and out of the house. She keeps talking about the fruit of my loins like we're doing something out of the Bible."

"Oh, man," said Deandre, with a shake of his head. "You going to be an old man before you get done with your kids."

"I can't even get my head around it," muttered Ray.

"Better get a big damn car," said Deandre.

"More like a school bus," sighed Ray.

Each man went silently back to his task. The job was lopping the low limbs off the trees to make room for the quick bottom cut that would topple the tree on harvest day. A fast harvest was a good harvest. Preparation was the key to a fast harvest.

The field had been planted with twenty rows of a hundred-fifty trees. Thanks to Deandre's apprentice bush hogging, the long grass and wildflowers between each row were cut down to ankle height. The trio worked within a few yards of each other, and the conversation helped pass the time. Big Tom, though, lagged a bit behind Ray and Deandre on account of his prosthetic.

Dawn was just then breaking into a clear November sky. A heavy frost lay on the grass. These were the busiest days on the farm. They had sixteen hours of work ahead of them, their second such "get 'er done" day in a row. It was left to Ken to manage the burns and after-parties, of which there were only two that week.

"I could actually see you two having that many kids," Big Tom called out. "I actually could. It would be a wild ride, but if anyone could do it, it would be you and Bonnie."

The cut limbs were left where they fell as the men moved from tree to tree. Bev and Myrna would be around later to drop off a hot lunch, and then they would gather up the tree cuttings for their wreath-making business. Every Christmas season Bev and Myrna made hundreds of wreaths and sold them to garden centers throughout the area. Long before they had teamed up with Ken to do catering for Big Burn, they were partnering with him on Christmas wreaths.

"Big Burn is going mammoth," continued Big Tom. "You're going to need some of those kids to help out around here before too long. But I got news for you, your days in the Pleasure Palace are numbered."

"Man, I can't even call it that anymore," said Ray, exasperated. "She's prayed the bad words right out of my mouth. It's my 'abode.' That's how I call it now, my 'abode,' because that's what she calls it."

Deandre made a sound like a whip cracking, prompting a chuckle from Big Tom.

"She's got you, man," laughed Big Tom. "You're working for her now. But you got to see the great deal you got. You're in with the boss's daughter, the one he's suddenly showering with attention."

"I know," said Ray. "Bonnie and Ken are going down father-daughter memory lane every chance she gets. It's driving Kim crazy. Probably Ken too, but he won't admit it. As good as Ken has been to us with Big Burn, he wasn't there for Bonnie. Every time they go down memory lane, him not being there for her comes right back up. Kim is fuming like I never seen."

"Oh, I know that," said Big Tom. "And Kim is driving Kelly crazy, too. I mean, they got a serious family feud building. And that ain't good for business. A house divided against itself cannot stand and neither can a business."

"You had to bring up Lincoln," said Ray.

"Well, he said it, and he was right," replied Big Tom. "Hey, D, you coming to Thanksgiving at Ken's with Bev and Myrna?"

"Yeah," said Deandre. "My folks are both on duty that day. I'm staying out here."

"Good, glad you're with us for the feast. Kelly is bringing her Texas-style sweet potatoes with pecans."

"Oh, I ain't missing that," said Deandre. "Bev and Myrna are making their goodies."

"Is Myrna making her awesome cheesecake?" asked Ray.

"Jamaican rum and coconut," said D. "It's already chilling in the fridge. She said it's the star of the dessert table."

"Yeah, it is," said Ray. "We love that cheesecake. Bonnie is making sausage dressing Siciliano. Save room for that. I'm going turkey hunting Wednesday morning for the bird."

"You going to get one?" asked Deandre.

"I do every year," answered Ray. "There's a flock on the mountain. I've already started calling them. They might just show up after we harvest these trees. So, yeah, I'll get my bird. And we'll have some venison. I got that doe last week. Meat will be ready from the butcher tomorrow. So we'll have fresh turkey and venison hunted right off the farm."

"Ricky Bobby!" yelled Deandre. "You da man."

Twenty-Six

"My boyfriend hunted this turkey," announced Bonnie, as she rubbed Ray's back. "He shot this turkey. And he cooked this turkey. And we are eating this turkey as thanks for the bounty of our land."

"My turkey got a bullet in it, man," said Deandre, spitting a small lead BB onto his fork.

"Oh, yeah, there it is," said Ray. "Sorry, D."

Deandre dropped the lead shotgun BB on his plate with a clink. Ray, sitting in between Bonnie and Deandre, leaned over to inspect Deandre's plate, smelled a familiar odor, and whispered, "You been smoking blunts?"

Grinning, Deandre whispered back: "It's Thanksgiving, man, so, yeah."

Ray shook his head. "Careful with that," he whispered to Deandre, who met his advice with a careless shrug.

"Yeah, watch out for the shotgun BBs in the turkey, guys," Ray announced to the group, as he pointed another one out to Deandre with the tip of his knife. "I got this gobbler with a head shot, but looks like a couple BBs hit midsection, so watch your bites. Don't break your teeth."

"What about the deer meat?" asked Deandre, poking his fork at the thick slice of venison in the center of his plate. "BBs in there?"

"Nothing to worry about in the venison. I took that doe with an arrow."

A Thanksgiving feast was spread out buffet-style in Ken's kitchen. The Big Burn crew, which included Bev and Myrna, had filled their plates and were now seated around Ken's dining room table. The men wore jackets and ties, the women, for the most part, dresses. Being that it was a Big Burn gathering on a chilly, grey November day, a fire was crackling in the fireplace.

Myrna, of course, wore her signature pants suit. As always, she was as flamboyant and colorful as her Jamaican heritage. And with Bev's expertise at braiding and beading, Myrna's hair was done up like a Caribbean queen.

It was a subdued gathering, with Bev, Myrna, and Kim the only ones drinking Chablis, the same as that served at the after-parties. Everyone one else had sparkling cider from an orchard over the mountain. Ken was the eldest and Deandre, the youngest. With no children present, it was more like an elaborate Big Burn weekly meeting than a family celebration.

"You killed a doe for Thanksgiving?" Kim asked Ray. She was twirling her wine glass and staring at it as though it was her own private oracle. Dressed in a sleeveless blue velvet cocktail number, Kim was seated with her back to the fire, at the end of the table opposite from Ken.

"Does are better eating than bucks," Ray said, giving Kim a side-eyed stare. "Got her right there in the Memory Garden."

Big Tom and Kelly exchanged glances. Kelly who was almost full term, wore a long-sleeve, black maternity blouse and an ankle-length grey wool skirt. Tom wore his church clothes, as did Bonnie and Ray. Ken in his tweed jacket and tie, was suddenly more interested in his plate of food than Ray and Kim's conversation.

"Oh, disgusting," said Kim, glaring at Ray. "I hope you cleaned it up."

"I dressed it out by my place," added Ray, "so no blood on the fancy path. I worked too hard on that to mess it up."

"Kelly, I'm enjoying your Texas sweet potatoes," Ken announced loudly, as he looked up from his plate. "They are perfect for this meal. Fit right in with the game Ray provided."

"Oh, thank you, Ken," said Kelly, as everyone but Kim nodded in agreement. "Sweet potatoes from your garden and the maple syrup came from my cousin Del. He bottles it off their farm near Staunton."

"Pecans are Virginia-grown too," added Big Tom.

"And, Myrna, what's with the zingy cranberry sauce?" asked Ken.

"That would be the rum, Ken," laughed Myrna. "Good Jamaican rum, strong and dark."

Ken chuckled, but pregnant Kelly raised her eyebrows with concern.

"Don't worry yourself, Kelly," assured Myrna, "I cooked it off, mostly flavoring."

Kelly nodded as she pushed the cranberry sauce further to the edge of her plate. "And, Kim," she added diplomatically, "your kale and arugula salad is delicious."

"Thank you," Kim said curtly. "Also right out of the garden. The leafy vegetables are still green and growing. Can't imagine what kind of fertilizer helps them do that."

Big Tom and Ken began shaking their heads as though warning Kim to tone it down. Everyone at the table knew she had been starving herself thin for her visit with Anthony. Her crash diet had made her crabby and sour for three weeks running. Salad was all she had on her plate, though she was well into her third extra-large glass of Chablis.

Ray cocked his head and was about to respond to Kim when Bonnie chimed in. "Oh, this is delicious, Ray," she crowed. "Fresh deer and turkey right off our land is a real treat for a girl from Vegas. Happy Thanksgiving, everybody. I feel just like a Pilgrim girl."

"But, Bonnie, I thought you were a Jesus girl," kidded Big Tom.

"I am, Tom," Bonnie replied. "Pilgrim girls were Jesus girls. And Pilgrim boys were Jesus boys, Finding their way to the New World with their Jesus by their side is what started America. They settled this country knowing that the Lord helps those who help themselves."

"Amen," said Ken. "Happy Thanksgiving. And, D, I just want to say we're glad to have you with us today and on the crew. We have been very impressed with your diligence. I don't think you know this, but I called your house last night and spoke to your dad. He was very happy to hear how well you're doing here at Big Burn. I know your folks are busy today, but I wanted you to know that they know we think you're doing a great job with us."

"Thanks, Ken," Deandre said gruffly, meeting Ken's eyes and nodding. Then he cleared his throat and said, "Y'all got me doing stuff I never thought I'd be doing."

"Well, you been on point since you got here," said Ray. "We just got to get you some coveralls at Tractor Supply, and you'll be all set."

"Coveralls from Tractor Supply, if Mama could see me now," laughed Deandre. "Let me just give props for my parents and all the rest of the folks on duty. My brother and sister are on duty, too — Navy and Air Force. Out of all my family, I'm the only one off today… eating this turkey with bullets in it."

Ray chuckled and gave Deandre a pat on the back, "Glad you're with us, D." Bev and Myrna beamed with pride.

Big Tom raised his glass, "To all the folks on duty all over the world who keep Thanksgiving safe for us all."

"Hear, hear," said Ken, as the group raised their glasses. "Ray and Deandre, you guys are set for that one-day burn we got going tomorrow?" he asked.

"Yeah, Ken," answered Ray. "We're good on that. Ceremony starts at two o'clock, they'll be mostly gone by eight, D and I got the burn and the after-party covered."

"And I'm on for prep and shroud," said Bonnie.

"Why do you keep calling it your land?" Kim asked, glaring at Bonnie.

"Excuse me?" asked Bonnie.

"Uh-oh," murmured Deandre, "here it comes," as Big Tom and Kelly nodded in alarm.

"Hush," Bev whispered urgently to Deandre.

"You can't just come in here with your fake prayers and gold dig your way into my family," muttered Kim, loud enough for all to hear. "You keep saying 'our' land like you're a Keeney. It's not your land. It's our land — Ken is my daddy, not yours. You're like a guest here, really you're an employee. It's not your land. It's not your place, so stop saying it is."

"Now hold on, Kimmy," said Ken, but Bonnie interrupted him.

"Kim, Ken is my daddy too," she said firmly. "I am not a Keeney, but Ken is my daddy. And I am thankful to be able to say that and for him owning up to it. Finally."

"How dare you say that," Kim practically spat her words at Bonnie.

"Excuse me, yes, I do dare say that because it's the truth. And if you can't tell the truth about your father to your father and the people who love him, why even bother calling it the truth? I'm twenty years old and it was only last month I found out for certain Ken is my father."

"He's not your father," Kim said, slamming her hand down on the table. "I'm the only one here who can call him Daddy."

"Getting real up in here," murmured Deandre, as Bev gave him her "hush up or else" look.

"Now, Kimmy," said Ken, who was again interrupted by Bonnie.

"Yes, he is too my daddy," she insisted. "I love Ken. I pray for Ken. And I forgive Ken for staying away from me and Aurie as much as he did. Being out here and seeing you and him and the farm and the Big Burn doings I understand more why he did it that way. But it still hurts, and I'm praying to Jesus for the wisdom to resolve that hurt. You might try praying to resolve your hurt. It works wonders."

"To hell with you and your praying," seethed Kim.

"Damn," Deandre repeated, giving Bev his "but I had to" look.

"I am sorry, Bonnie," Ken, announced loudly as all eyes shifted to him, "that it still hurts. You came here and showed me my mistake, a dreadful mistake. I needed that. The best gift a man's children can give him is their truth about him… because a good man will listen to his children above all else. You are right that I should have owned up to it long ago. I thought I was. I told myself by sending checks I was, and I got your mom to agree with me. But it wasn't true because I didn't ask you. I didn't think of you like I should have. I wasn't honest with you. I apologize. And thank you for forgiving me. I'm mad at myself about it — been that way for a while. But I'm thankful you're here. I'm thankful you're my daughter. I'm thankful you're with Ray. And I'm thankful we are all together now as a family, and we are a family. Everyone in this room is family — the Big Burn family."

"A screwed up family," declared Kim.

"Kim, honey," said Ken sadly.

"Don't 'Kim honey' me," Kim hissed.

"Oh, girl, that's no way to be on Thanksgiving," chided Bev. "We are a family. And, Ken, I appreciate you saying it that way. I know Myrna does. We feel like you been brotherly to us since we met, what twenty years ago when we started doing wreaths."

"Yeah, twenty years ago," said Ken. "And that's how I feel, Bev. No one at this table is an employee, Kim. And understand this, now I've got two daughters. That's twice as good."

"Well, then excuse me, loving family," Kim said bitterly, and she went into the kitchen to refill her wine glass.

Ken watched her leave and then said, "Big Burn is a family that's a business and business that's a family. We all make mistakes, we just got to back each other up when we do and forgive each other. Family comes first."

"Wait, your mother was named Aurie?" Ray asked Bonnie. "You never told me that. My mother's name was Lori."

"Lori and Aurie watching over us from heaven," said Bonnie.

"Yeah, Lori Raines Wells was my mom, and my dad was Jimmy — Jimmy Wells. Wow, that was weird. That's the first time I said their names out loud in a long, long time."

"Aurie Betts was my mother," said Bonnie. "And she never told me who my dad was. I guess she thought me having Ken as a once a year uncle was better than me having him as a once a year father."

Tom and Kelly both nodded. "It's not a bad day to remember those who have moved on," said Tom. "All of them, heroes or not."

"Lori and Jimmy," said Ray. "Ain't going to lie, back then in '92, they were already partying like it was 1999, and that was that. Crashed that car and Aunt Nancy took me in."

"Nancy and Trey," added Big Tom. "I ain't thought about my dad in a long time, either. But I do remember him carving up a turkey a couple times."

"They're watching us from heaven too," said Bonnie.

"This is ridiculous," seethed Kim, as she returned to the table. "It's Thanksgiving not Prayergiving. She comes in here with her fake Jesus, and everyone joins in to be fake righteous just like her."

All eyes turned to Kim, with Ken's expression bearing the most sadness. An awkward silence settled over the gathering for a couple minutes. Finally, Bev spoke up with an observation. "You know, Ken," she said, "The tree harvest is so much work, there might be a better way to do it next year.”

“What do you mean?” asked Ken, suddenly stiffening. No matter the day, time, or circumstance, Ken Keeney was like a bloodhound for business. If he scented an entrepreneurial opportunity, he wanted to run it down.

“More wreaths,” said Bev. “Don’t harvest the trees, use them to make wreaths. Because the biggest limitation we have for our wreaths is how many branches we get off the bottom cut. But if we use branches from the whole tree, there’s no limit.”

“A lot of folks just buy a fresh wreath. More of those out there than trees,” added Deandre as he closely eyeballed the chunk of turkey on the end of his fork.

Ken learned forward in his chair, while Big Tom and Ray nodded agreeably.

“We can get enough branches off a tree to make three or four wreaths at $15 each, wholesale,” continued Bev. “And I can get the wholesale accounts. By myself I can make five or six wreaths an hour. I get some people trained up on it, like D and Bonnie, and we can put out twenty-five or more an hour.”

“Those are good numbers,” agreed Ken. “So we just stop harvesting whole trees and harvest branches for wreaths, is that it?”

“That’s what I’m thinking,” said Bev.

“That ain’t bad thinking,” said Big Tom. “Especially if we’re doing winter cremations next year.”

Ken nodded, “Good point,” he said. “Harvesting a parcel of trees is almost four solid weeks of work for all hands. That’s a lot of burns we’d have to delay.” Then he looked across the table to Kim. Hoping to pull her back into the conversation, he asked: "What do you think, Kim?"

"I think Bonnie is a slut," Kim said staring blankly at the wine glass in front of her. "I think Ray is a slut. No surprise there, birds of a feather. I think sluts are bad for business. And I think I am done with this dinner and this Thanksgiving. I'm going to my room. Tomorrow cannot come fast enough. Daddy, I can take a $200 cab ride to the airport or you can drive me. Your choice. I want to leave here tomorrow morning at seven o'clock. I am packed and ready to go. And this is goodbye to you all. Maybe for a long time. Maybe forever. That's what I'm thankful for."

With that, Kim left. And everyone at the table sat in stunned silence.

Twenty-Seven

"You sure you want to do this," said Ray as he watched Bonnie un-button her blouse. "This is kind of wild even for you."

"No, I'm not sure, Ray," said Bonnie, unhooking her bras. Then, nude from the waist up and standing beside Kim's bed, she explained: "I'm not sure at all. I have prayed and prayed to Jesus for wisdom on this because I know it's... naughty."

Ray, still wearing all his clothes, said, "I'd say it's more than naughty. You're getting back at your sister and pulling me into it."

"Well, you are in it, too, Ray," Bonnie said. "She called us both sluts. You heard her. She lied on us in front everybody we love. We're not sluts, we're us, and there's nothing wrong with us. I've done a lot of thinking on this."

"Honey, I agree you have."

"She's the liar," continued Bonnie. "She's the sinner. Not us."

"Well, she did lie on us," agreed Ray, as he pulled off his work vest and unbuttoned his shirt. "Because we have never been slutty — well, not with each other."

"That's right. We did the forty days and forty nights. We prayed for each other because we love each other. That's not slutty. Getting married and having a whole lot of babies is Jesus's plan for us. I just know it is."

"I like Jesus's plan for us," said Ray.

"Good, let's go," said Bonnie as she kicked off her sheepskin boots and unbuttoned her jeans.

"But, honey," added Ray, "Us doing it in her bed to get back at her is also a sin."

"Technically, Ray, you are correct," said Bonnie, who, now fully nude, had seated herself on Kim's immaculately made-up bed. "But we can do it in her bed and then afterwards pray to Jesus for forgiveness and then we're forgiven and everything is okay. So, we're just sinners for a little while, and then we go right back to being cleansed in the eyes of the Lord."

"I'm pretty sure that's not exactly right," said Ray, who, wearing only his boots and jeans, stood with his arms folded.

"Well, what is right?"

"You put me through it those forty days and forty nights," continued Ray. "And I was in and out of that pond hundreds of times, but we never gave in to temptation. We are not sinners. But as soon as we do it on your sister's bed for revenge, we'll be sinners. I say we just go downstairs and do it on the couch. Kind of naughty, kind of crazy. We can be us without stooping to Kim's level. Leave the sinning to her."

"Well, you do have a point, Right Way Ray," sighed Bonnie. "Oh, it is hard to be a Jesus girl! But my sister lied on me and you, and she needs to be taught a lesson. I mean, the Bible says turn the other cheek, well, I'm ready to turn my other cheeks every which way all over her bed, and we can turn your other cheeks all over it, too. We can just roll our other cheeks around and around and around all over Kimmy's precious bed in Kimmy's special room where she says I am forbidden to go. Because guess what, I ain't letting Kimmy forbid me from nothing on this farm. Ken is my daddy, too. It's as much my farm as it is hers."

"Well, that is standing up for yourself," said Ray, enjoying the sight of Bonnie, without a stitch of clothes on, getting herself all riled up. "Jesus ain't against standing up for yourself."

"That is correct," Bonnie said, as she patted the bedspread beside her. "Jesus stood up for himself and us, and look where it got him, he's the Savior of the world."

"And he does forgive sinners," continued Ray. "And I have sure been a sinner before, and I've put in all this time to not be one, and here you are tempting me... Oh, it is hard to be a Jesus man."

Just then the Big Burn Funeral Services office phone rang downstairs. Loud and jarring. Ray and Bonnie locked eyes.

"You better get that," said Ray. "You're supposed to be watching the phones."

"It might be Daddy," Bonnie said as she jumped off the bed. "He said he'd call from the airport after Kim's plane took off."

Nude, she trotted downstairs without hesitation. Ray watched her, admiring not just her physical gifts but more the grace with which she wielded them. Ray saw then and there Bonnie's connection to Jesus: She was beautiful because she lived with unquestioning faith — her beauty was her faith, her faith was her beauty.

And he had the terrible feeling they were on the verge of ruining it.

Ray, still half-dressed, looked around Kim's bedroom, realizing he'd never seen it before, never been near it. Heck, this was the first time he'd been upstairs in Ken's house. It kind of reminded him of when he was in high school and he'd sneak over to his girlfriend's house when her parents were out. But this was his girlfriend's sister's room. Something wasn't right.

The phone stopped ringing. He heard Bonnie's melodic phone greeting, "Big Burn Funeral Services."

Ray scanned Kim's bedroom, her orderly, feminine sanctuary, and realized how deeply personal this room was for her. One of the walls was filled floor to ceiling with photos. Most of them were of just her and her mother — baby photos, toddler photos, birthday cake photos. Karen Keeney was a beautiful woman who loved her daughter. That was evident. Ken was in a lot of photos with her and Kim. What was also evident in every photo was their family pride and happiness. But then there was half a wall of photos of just Ken and Kim. Each one tinged with sadness.

Right there in front of him was the sight of twenty years of Kim's motherless life. Downstairs on the phone was the sound of twenty years of Bonnie's fatherless life. And they were sisters, with more in common than either could admit.

"Nope, not here," Ray muttered into the empty room. "Jesus, I know you hear me. This ain't us. We ain't doing this. Thanks for setting me straight."

Ray bent over and picked up his shirt and vest, then he scooped up Bonnie's clothes.

He was in the hallway as she came bounding up the stairs, her eyes wide. "That was Tom," she said. "The midwife is there. Kelly and the baby are in distress. They're going to the hospital."

Twenty-Eight

DADDY

WE ARE AT CULPEPER GENERAL HOSPITAL

KELLY AND BABY IN DISTRESS

BONNIE

Ken Keeney read the hand-scrawled note taped in the middle of the farmhouse front door and felt his insides go liquid. It was the same feeling he'd had when the doctor at Culpeper General had told him Karen had died.

His shoulders sagged as he set the heavier of Kim's two suitcases on the porch. Kim, who was carrying the lighter suitcase, walked up behind him. "Oh, no," she gasped. "Kelly, oh, Kelly."

"Let's go," Ken said grimly.

Kim, face puffy from crying, eyes rimmed with tear-smudged mascara, nodded, set down her suitcase, and turned immediately for Ken's truck, with her father following at her heels.

Twenty-Nine

"Baby's gone," Big Tom whispered hoarsely. "Girl. Stillborn."

"No," said Ray. "No, oh, Tom."

"Kelly's okay," he said wearily, his voice trailing off when he added: "No complications…"

"Oh, Kelly," said Bonnie. She and Ray were standing in the hospital waiting room. Ray had his arm around Bonnie.

"Baby never drew a breath," whispered Big Tom, looking up at the ceiling, as though he could see right through it all the way up into the house of God himself.

Bonnie put her hands to her face and burst into tears. "Oh, no, I can't believe it, I can't believe it. I've been praying so hard."

Ray pulled Big Tom into a hug. "Oh, man, I'm so, so sorry," he said.

Big Tom couldn't lift his arms to hug him back.

"A girl," Bonnie sobbed.

"Kelly's got her," said Big Tom. "She's got her there all wrapped up like she's, you know, just sleeping." At that, Big Tom crumpled. Ray caught him and guided him to a seat on a three-person couch, where Deandre, Bev, and Myrna were seated. Deandre and Myrna stood up to make room for Big Tom.

"Oh, man," sobbed Big Tom, as he sat with his other hand shading his eyes, "I got blown up in Iraq. This is ten times worse."

At this, Myrna and Deandre went behind the couch and put hands on Big Tom's shoulders. No words. Just comforting touch. He nodded a greeting through his sobs. They were somber. But Big Tom weeping was too much. The ladies went all-in teary. Deandre, too. Nothing sadder than seeing a strong man crying his heart out for his teeny, little baby.

"I couldn't help her," sobbed Big Tom. "Couldn't do nothing. No one could. She just — her little baby heart just stopped. Doctors can't say why."

"I'm going to go in and see Kelly," whispered Bonnie.

"Yeah," nodded Big Tom, "she needs you. I'm going to call her parents and her sister. They're standing by in Dallas." Big Tom squeezed his eyes shut as if forcing himself to stop seeing what was happening. "This is going to be awful," he said, his voice breaking. "They were so excited for this visit, now it's..."

From behind him, Myrna rubbed his back, while Bev, beside him, rubbed his arm. Deandre sat side-saddle on the end of the couch.

"Just take your time, man," said Ray, offering Big Tom a handkerchief from his back pocket. "Take your time. We're here."

Big Tom took the handkerchief and buried his face in it. Bonnie had fished a tissue out of her shoulder bag and was dabbing her eyes dry.

"Bonnie, you go see how Kelly is doing," said Ray. "We'll stay out here with Tom."

Bonnie took a deep breath. "Okay," she exhaled, "where are they?"

"Room 221," Big Tom said without lifting the handkerchief from his face.

"Okay," said Bonnie.

The room was dark and silent when Bonnie pushed the door open and slid inside. The lights were off. The shades were drawn, with only a tiny glow of daylight framing their edges. Kelly sat upright, with the head of the bed adjusted up like a recliner. She was still as a statue with a little blanketed bundle in her arms.

"Hi sweetie," said Bonnie in a sugary whisper. "I just came to see how you're doing."

"We're okay," said Kelly, her voice quavering. "She's sleeping. Rose is sleeping."

Bonnie padded quietly over to the bed. Kelly didn't move. She was cradling the baby in her arms, staring down at her dead daughter's face.

"Is that her name, Rose?" whispered Bonnie, as she got herself seated at the edge of the bed.

"Yeah, Rose," sighed Kelly, without looking up. "I had other names because we didn't know…" Kelly gulped down a sob. "But then I knew I wanted to name her after a flower. We got our rose garden, and now she's my Rose."

"Rose is a beautiful name."

"Yeah, she's so pretty. She's sleeping."

"She's sleeping?" whispered Bonnie.

"Yeah, she's sleeping," Kelly whispered. "She's such a good baby. She's sleeping and sleeping."

"Oh, she is a good baby."

Bonnie sat quietly as Kelly admired her lifeless baby. She was smoothing her tufty hair over and over.

"I'm not going to cry," whispered Kelly, "because that will wake her. She's such a good baby, sleeping for Mama."

"I know, I know."

"I love her so much."

"I know you do, honey. She is so lucky to have you for her mama."

"I loved her the second I felt she was there."

"I know, I know you did."

"She was my Little Peanut, just a sweet, tiny, little thing, but she was mine. I felt her inside me. She was in my heart, I felt her every minute she was alive."

"I know, honey, I know."

"And she got bigger and bigger and stronger and fussy with her kicking."

"We felt those kicks. She was so strong."

"She was so strong. And she got to know her Mama and her Daddy. We talked to her all the time."

"Yes, you did. She heard you. She knew you loved her. She knew her parents loved her."

"Oh, she did, she did. She knew we loved her. She was ready. She was coming to be with us… and then she just stopped." Kelly looked up at Bonnie, her eyes filling with tears, her voice breaking. "She just stopped. I don't know why she just stopped. She just stopped."

"I don't know either, honey. I don't know."

"Why did she just stop?" sobbed Kelly, and then in a deep wail of anguish, "Why?"

Bonnie rubbed Kelly's leg as she sobbed and sobbed while clutching Rose. Bonnie was in tears. Kelly was in tears. Finally Bonnie asked, "Can I see her?"

Kelly nodded and passed Rose over to Bonnie. "Oh, she's so pretty," said Bonnie. "Hi… hi, sweetie." And Bonnie realized she would soon be anointing Rose and wrapping her in a tiny, tiny shroud. "Look at her little fingers and fingernails," said Bonnie as she caressed Rose's tiny hands, which were limp and floppy and grey blue. Her lips were blue. Her face was ashen. "She's a gorgeous baby, honey."

"She is, she is."

Bonnie undid the blanket, saw there was no diaper. "Pretty little toes," she said, holding the lifeless foot. "Look at those cute little baby toes."

Kelly nodded.

Bonnie rewrapped the swaddling blanket and handed Baby Rose back. "Are you okay, honey? She's sleeping. Maybe you want to close your eyes and get some rest. You've been through a lot. You lay down with your baby and sleep. I'll stay here and say a prayer for you and your baby. Here, I'll lower your bed."

"Okay," Kelly said meekly. "Okay, I'll just snuggle here with Rose."

"You do that, honey," Bonnie said as she lowered the bed and watched Kelly stretch out, clutching her baby. "I'll just be here praying for you and Rose."

"Okay," Kelly whispered, rolling over on her side to stare at her baby.

Bonnie silently prayed for Rose, Kelly, and Tom, but then just as Kelly was dozing off, a newborn in the next room squalled as loud as if it were right there with them. Kelly woke with a start. "Rose?" she asked. "Rose, is that you? Mama's here. Mama's here."

But Rose wasn't crying. She was an inert bundle of silence. Kelly rested her hand on her dead baby. Her arm was trembling. She buried her face in the bed, stifling her cries.

Bonnie watched helplessly as her friend struggled to accept that the daughter she had loved and nurtured in her womb for so many hopeful months would never cry, never breathe, never open her eyes. Her daughter was gone. With the absolute finality of death, gone.

Just then there was a soft knock at the door. "Sorry to bother you," came the authoritative whisper. A bespectacled, grey-haired nurse pushed the door slightly ajar. "Do you need a little more time?"

"What do you mean?" whispered Bonnie, as she moved quickly to the door, placing her body in front of the intrusion.

"We're processing Mrs. Wells' discharge," continued the nurse with only half her face showing through the crack in the doorway, "but we can come back if she needs more time."

"She's going to need more time, yes. They're going to need more time."

"That's fine," agreed the nurse, in a businesslike tone. "We'll be back in a couple hours. Mrs. Wells can have that time, but then we'll need to take the baby, and Mr. and Mrs. Wells can go home and get some rest."

"Wait, you're going to take the baby from her?"

"We have to process the death through the morgue. It's a legal requirement this hospital must uphold. So, yes, we will take the baby before the discharge. I'm sorry, but it's required by law. Our bereavement counselor has apprised Mr. Wells of next steps. I suggest you and he come to an understanding about this with Mrs. Wells. But for now, let's let her rest."

The door closed. Bonnie looked back at Kelly cuddling her dead baby in her cocoon of grief. She couldn't imagine Kelly surrendering her baby to a morgue. For a long time she stood at the door, waiting for Kelly to doze off. There were hospital sounds in the hallway. Doors were opening. Muted conversations. It was midday, the Friday after Thanksgiving. Lunches were being distributed. Healthy babies were thriving on the maternity ward. Joyous parents were cooing and murmuring. But not in that room. Bonnie couldn't stop thinking about those two hideous words the nurse had uttered: the morgue.

Finally, Kelly's regular breathing told Bonnie she had fallen asleep. Quietly, Bonnie slipped out. Two steps down the hallway she saw Big Tom. "Hey," he said, "Kim and your dad are here."

"Kim?"

"I'm going to sit with Kelly," he said.

"And Rose," said Bonnie.

"And Rose," agreed Big Tom. "Go check in with your dad and Kim.

I'm just going to sit with Kelly and Rose until you guys come get us. It's all I can do right now."

"Why is Kim here?"

"Just go check with them."

Bonnie nodded and hurried down the hallway. But when she turned the corner into the waiting room, there was Kim, and she was hugging Ray. Just those two remained in the waiting area. Everybody else was gone. Her dad was nowhere to be seen.

"Hey, honey," Ray said sheepishly, "look who's here."

"Kim, what are you..."

"Bonnie, I am so, so sorry for everything," said Kim, somewhat awkwardly as she stepped back from Ray. "I feel awful for Kelly and Tom, but I'm also very, very sorry for what I said yesterday about you and Ray. Please accept my apology."

"Okay," Bonnie said defensively, arms crossed. "What about Anthony and Tasmania? And where's Daddy?" she asked.

"Daddy is with D," answered Kim. "They're taking care of the ceremony we had lined up for today, which starts in about two hours. Prep and shroud, after-party, everything. Bev and Myrna are getting the food together. They're going to make some extra for you guys and bring it by Tom and Kelly's."

"What do you mean for us guys?" asked Bonnie, feeling annoyed that Kim had butted in so effectively.

"We're helping Tom and Kelly," explained Ray. "We'll get them home. Kim has got it all sorted out with the hospital."

"That's right," added Kim. "You guys are taking Tom and Kelly and the baby home to their house tonight. That baby is never going to the morgue. She's never going in a body bag. She's Kelly's daughter, and she's going home with her Mama," said Kim, tearing up. "And we are going to take care of her and Kelly and Tom to help get through this as best they can."

"Kim knows the hospital folks," explained Ray. "And they gave us the okay. We'll get the baby home with Kelly—"

"Rose," said Bonnie. "Her name is Rose. Kelly named her Rose."

"Oh, Rose," sniffled Kim. "That's a pretty name. Well, officially the body will be released to me in my capacity as vice president of Big Burn Funeral Services, but instead of me taking her out in a body bag, Kelly will take her out bundled in her arms. They'll get a wheelchair for her. Ray can drive them home in Tom's truck. You can follow in Ray's truck. We'll have the baby's cremation tomorrow afternoon. They can have a night with her at their house. Bev and Myrna are going to drop by some food, and they'll get Kelly's church friends to drop by with casseroles. You and Ray can help them with whatever they need. We'll have everything ready at the farm tomorrow for Rose — to send her on."

"To heaven," said Bonnie.

"To heaven, yes, to heaven," agreed Kim.

"But what about Anthony and Tasmania?" asked Bonnie, her tone softening.

Kim sighed and looked directly at Bonnie. "Daddy and I had a long talk on the drive to and from the airport, about stuff we probably should have been talking about for a long, long time — my mom, her death, how I'd grown up at Holtwood and not on the farm. He told me about him and your mom and you. He feels bad about keeping it from both of us, but also trying to now pull the good out of it. 'Reconnected family' is how he said it."

Watching Kim as she spoke, Bonnie felt something shift. No longer did she see confident, professional, bossy Kim, but for the first time she saw vulnerable Kim. Standing before her was a woman who was once a young girl, who had lost her mother, only to be sent off to boarding school, far away from her farm and her dad. It was the worst kind of hurt, old and buried.

"Holtwood must have been hard for you," said Bonnie.

"I cried and cried the first couple of months," said Kim, nodding at the memory. "But then I made friends and it was better. At least I've always told myself that."

Bonnie leaned into Ray for a hug. Her memory flashed through special moments she and her mom had shared.

"Anyway," added Kim, "I rescheduled my flight. Anthony was disappointed, but he understood. I'll be with him for three weeks — the two weeks before Christmas and then coming back first week in January. I'm actually kind of relieved to slow things down."

Bonnie nodded. "I thought you couldn't change the ticket."

"I couldn't," said Kim. "I thought it was too expensive. But Daddy paid for it. He said, 'We have to get this right, today. Family comes first. You have a sister. Bonnie is your little sister. You have to get it right with her.'"

"He said that?" asked Bonnie.

Kim nodded solemnly. "And then we saw the note on the door, and it's just become a terrible day. I'm so sorry, Bonnie," said Kim, her lips trembling. "I been crying all morning. I was awful to you and

Ray yesterday. You're my sister. You're my little sister. I'm supposed to help you, not hurt you. Please forgive me."

Weeping afresh, Bonnie pulled Kim into a hug. "We are sisters," she said. "We are sisters. You're my big sister. And we're sisters with Kelly, and she lost her baby."

Ray stood by as Kim and Bonnie hugged and hugged and cried. Just then a mother with a newborn bundled in her arms came down the hall in a wheelchair pushed by the same grey-haired nurse who had knocked at Kelly's door. The father, huge bag of baby items slung over his shoulder, followed close behind. They watched her in silence. "We have to get Kelly, Tom, and Rose out of here," said Kim.

Bonnie nodded. "Yeah, you're right. I'll go talk to them. Does Tom know about the discharge plan?"

"He does," said Kim. "But you and Ray should talk them both through it."

"Pray them through it," added Bonnie.

"That too," agreed Kim.

"Ray, come with me," said Bonnie.

"Oh, no," said Ray, shaking his head, "I don't know about that."

"Ray Wells," said Bonnie, with a very firm tone, "We are going together to support Kelly and Tom in their hour of need, and we are going to shower Baby Rose with the love she deserves."

"Okay," said Ray. "Okay."

Kim looked at her watch. "I'm going down to the morgue," she said. "I got to check on the death certificate. Let me know when Kelly is ready to leave, and I'll get her a nurse with a wheelchair."

"Thank you, Kim," said Bonnie, looking directly at Kim, "for all this. Thank you so much. You're a wonder worker."

Ray nodded. "You're making this bad day not so bad," he said. "Thank you."

"You're welcome," said Kim. "We'll get through this. Tom and Kelly will get through this. We're a family. We'll help each other through it."

"Okay," said Bonnie. "We'll be with Kelly, Tom, and Rose."

Kim went down the hall toward the elevators while Ray and Bonnie went the opposite direction toward Kelly's room. "Okay, can I just say thank God we didn't do it on her bed," exclaimed Bonnie as soon as Kim was out of earshot.

"Thank God is right," said Ray. "We would have been sluts if we had gone through with it."

"I know, I know," agreed Bonnie. "Let's not talk about it ever again."

"Never again," agreed Ray, as they stopped in front of Room 221.

Bonnie knocked softly and pushed in. Big Tom was in a chair he had pulled up close to Kelly's bed. He was holding Baby Rose. Kelly was laying on her side, watching him. "Hey, guys," whispered Bonnie. "Is it okay if we come in? Ray wants to meet Baby Rose."

Big Tom and Kelly nodded, each with nearly the exact same expression of exhaustion, grief, and bewilderment. Ray went to Big Tom, who silently handed over the bundled body of his dead daughter.

"She's sleeping," Kelly murmured, still laying on her side.

Ray looked down into Baby Rose's ashen face. He couldn't hide his shock. With all eyes in the room watching him, Ray let loose the waterworks. Tears ran freely down the sides of his face. But then noting the beauty of her tiny baby features, the miracle that she was, even in death, he murmured over and over, "Hi Peanut, hi, hi." And then through his tears, a "Right Way Ray" smile couldn't help but curl up at the corner of his lips. "Baby Rose, you are so beautiful," he said.

Bonnie moved to sit side-saddle on the foot of Kelly's bed. She laid a hand on her leg. "How you doing, honey?" she asked.

"Tired," said Kelly.

"Okay," said Bonnie. "You feeling like you want to head home? Ray and I can get you guys home."

"What about Baby Rose?" she asked, with a panicked expression.

"Baby Rose can come, too."

"Kim fixed it?" asked Big Tom.

"Yes, she did," repeated Bonnie. "My sister is a wonder worker, and she's got you guys discharged to take Baby Rose home. You can carry her home in your arms. They got a wheelchair for Kelly and Rose, we'll put you guys in Tom's truck. Ray can drive you home."

Just then the newborn in the next room began squalling. The sound came right through the wall causing Kelly and Big Tom to flinch simultaneously. After a few moments of pained listening, Kelly spoke up: "In the delivery room when I finally had my last push, and they got her out, it was just silence. Nothing."

Big Tom stared up at the ceiling as he relived those terrible moments. Ray wiped his face with his shirtsleeve. Bonnie rubbed

Kelly's leg.

"The doctors were silent," continued Kelly. "The room was silent. Everything. Everyone. All quiet. The hospital chaplain was there to baptize her, but she wasn't alive, so he didn't baptize her. He just said a prayer for us and left." At this Kelly erupted in deep wrenching sobs. Her entire body was trembling. No one spoke. Ray quietly handed Baby Rose back to Big Tom. Time passed. After a long while Kelly's sobs subsided.

"Come on," said Bonnie. "Let's get you guys home where it's quiet. Get you in your own bed. You and Tom can show Baby Rose her room."

Kelly raised her eyes to Bonnie's at the mention of Baby Rose's room. Bonnie took note. "Come on, honey," she said. "She's got such a pretty room. We worked so hard to make it pretty for her."

"Oh, we did, we did," sniffed Kelly. "Her room is so pretty."

"Let's go take Baby Rose home to her room," agreed Bonnie. "You and Tom can spend the night with her. Just you three in her pretty little room. You can be there together."

"Just us three, me and Tom and Rose in her room, like I dreamed it would be," said Kelly as she reached for Baby Rose.

"Just like you dreamed," agreed Bonnie. "And Ray and I can stay in my room. We'll be there for you if you need us."

"Okay," said Kelly, as Big Tom nodded in agreement. "That does sound better than here."

"Ray," said Bonnie, "go find Kim. Let's get a wheelchair. Let's get everyone home."

Nodding, Ray slipped out of the room. And as he strode down the hospital hall, he thought about how lucky he was to have Bonnie, Kim, and Kelly in his life. Three words popped into his head: "Thank you, Jesus."

Thirty

The lights in Rose's room were off. A feeble November glow came through the half-drawn curtains in the dormer window. Outside, twilight was darkening into night. Big Tom was sleeping, his deep breathing nearly a snore. He was on the mattress of his and Kelly's bed. Ray had cleared a place for it on the floor and brought it in. Big Tom's wheelchair was set beside the mattress. Ray had brought that in, too.

But Big Tom's prosthetic wasn't in the room. It was next door, in his bedroom, standing next to his changing chair and table. He had asked Ray to set it there, along with the socks and sleeves he used to fit his leg into and out of his prosthetic. It had surprised Ray when Big Tom had asked him to take it away. "You sure?" he asked.

"I'll just go with the crutches and the chair for a couple days," said Big Tom. "Putting the prosthetic on is — well, I'm just not up for it right now. That's all."

So, Big Tom slept in his dead daughter's room, wheelchair nearby, crutches leaning against the wall. It was the first time since he'd worn his prosthetic that it wasn't either on him or within arm's reach.

Kelly was there, too. She wasn't sleeping. As exhausted as she was, something told her closing her eyes and dreaming would break her heart. She kept herself awake by humming to her baby. She was standing in front of the full-length mirror she had bought at a yard sale in the summer — the moment she saw that mirror, she knew it would be perfect for her baby's room.

Barefoot, wearing her nightgown, she had showered and washed her hair. She was holding Baby Rose in a blanketed bundle. And while she felt clean and fresh, Baby Rose had grown stiff with rigor mortis. But just then that didn't matter to Kelly. For as long as the light allowed her, she was just standing there willing herself awake, watching herself rocking her baby in her baby's bedroom mirror, the one she had bought at a yard sale in town.

Because she knew it was perfect.

Thirty-One

"She's going to look so tiny on that big cooker grill," Bonnie told Deandre as she placed Baby Rose's shrouded body on the prep table. They were in the Metal Barn, which was still cold from the overnight temperature plunge. Outside it was a bright November Saturday. Inside the Metal Barn, it was dim and cold.

"I got the logs piled at the center," said Deandre. "That's what Ray said Big Tom wanted, and it's all pine. He wants it to blaze up big time."

"That's what Tom wanted?" asked Bonnie. She was wiping oil from her hands with paper towels. Baby Rose was so small, she had just anointed her with her bare hands.

"That's what Ray said he wanted, a big burn," replied Deandre.

"A big burn?" asked Bonnie, surprised.

"A really big burn — big, fiery, and fast."

"Well, if that's what Tom wanted," said Bonnie, as she scooped up Baby Rose's stiff shrouded body. Deandre was holding the door for Bonnie. "Come on, let's get her down there," she said, blinking to adjust to the daylight. "You drive the hearse while I hold her."

"Huh, me drive the hearse."

"It's that kind of a day, isn't it?"

"Yep, all messed up."

They climbed in the hearse and drove in silence to the cooker. Bonnie was lost in thought. There was no need for the viewing bier. There was no stretcher. There would be no pallbearers. There was only a tiny, tiny shrouded body on a massive iron grill. That alone was heartbreaking. Bonnie glanced down at Baby Rose, wrapped like a caterpillar in a cocoon. That innocent little baby, loved by so many, was about to leave them forever. All the hope and love they had poured into her future was gone. She felt like crying but was just then too worn out.

When they arrived at the cooker, she set her down and quickly turned away. "This is going to be so hard for Kelly to see," she said.

"I'll stay here and make sure she's okay," said Deandre. "My parents are driving up from Petersburg and picking up Bev and Myrna. I want to be here when they arrive."

"In the catering van?" queried Bonnie with a forehead wrinkle.

"Oh, hell, no," said Deandre, then seeing Bonnie flinch, he corrected himself, "oh, heck no. The Sergeant Major ain't riding in Bev's old catering van. He's got his Grand Cherokee. He'll drive them in that."

"Oh, that's good," said Bonnie. "This is hard on all of us. It's good your parents can be here with us and for you."

"Mom suggested it last night when I called them," said Deandre. "Aunt Bev and Myrna thought it was a good idea. I checked with Ken and he said it was okay."

"We need to lean on each other right now," agreed Bonnie.

"I got my funeral clothes in my car. I'll change up in the pavilion. Everything will be ready when you guys get here."

"Okay, D," said Bonnie. "Thanks for being here with her. It will mean a lot to Kelly and Big Tom that you're here watching over her."

Thirty-Two

The flag was the first thing that caught Big Tom's eye. He recognized it as the classroom-sized American flag they kept tacked on the wall in the pavilion. It must have been Deandre who had draped it over Baby Rose. Seeing it on the cooker put Big Tom's heart in an iron-fisted squeeze.

The second thing that caught Big Tom's eye was the cascade of roses — yellow, red, white, pink — covering the cooker from end to end. Baby Rose was surrounded by a cloud of roses. Her pyre looked as festive as a float in a parade.

"Roses," murmured Kelly. "Look at all the roses."

They were in Big Tom's truck. Ray was driving with Bonnie alongside in the passenger seat. Big Tom and Kelly shared the backseat. Behind them, Ken was driving Kim in his truck. Reverend Carr, the pastor from Tom and Kelly's church, was by himself, bringing up the rear. Ray parked along the driveway by the viewing bier. Deandre's father's Grand Cherokee was already there.

Big Tom turned in his seat and saw his wife's anguish melt into wonder at the sight of the roses. "Had to be Myrna," he said, as that familiar iron fist squeezed even harder.

Deandre, jacket and tie, was standing at attention, like a military escort. Bev and Myrna were there, too. They were waiting beside a small semi-circle of plastic folding chairs. A well-dressed couple stood next to them. Deandre's parents. Deandre's dad wore a suit under an Army green trench coat. His mom, like Bev and Myrna, wore a dark dress under a full-length winter coat.

Bonnie opened her door, went straight to Deandre and wrapped him in a hug. "Oh, thank you, D, for doing this," she said. "The flag and the roses, where did you find them?"

"It's the flag from the pavilion," Deandre explained. "I saw it and knew it was just right for Baby Rose. Then Bev and Myrna came by with all these roses."

"We went to three stores before we had enough," said Myrna.

"Good thinking on the flag, D," said Ray, hugging Deandre. "The pyre looks good." Then dropping his voice he asked, "You got extra accelerants in there?"

"A whole rack of them," whispered Deandre. "Just like you said."

Ray nodded.

Kelly walked up and hugged Deandre. "Thank you, D," she said. "Thank you for thinking of this for us. I'll never forget this."

Deandre, holding back tears, nodded gravely.

But Big Tom remained in his truck. His crutches were propped on the seat next to him. He wore his best suit, white shirt, dark blue tie. Bonnie had pinned the one leg of his pants up so it didn't flap. He had no overcoat, just the suit. But he didn't even feel like he was wearing clothes. All he felt was that familiar iron fist around his heart.

It had been there in Iraq. He thought he'd left it there. Hadn't felt it since before he'd been blown up. And now it was back. Seeing that little body, that little flag, on came the iron-fisted squeeze, just like in Iraq for so many brothers and sisters. What he thought was buried in the past, was right there all over again.

Big Tom put his face to his hands. His little baby was dead and under a flag. The dam burst. There was no stopping it. Grief poured out of him like a flood. Big Tom wept like a man who couldn't understand why he had given more than everything.

While he was doing that, Bev and Myrna got big hugs from Bonnie and Kelly for the rose decorations. They introduced Deandre's parents to handshakes and thank-yous. Ken, Kim, and Reverend Carr walked up. "Exceptional job here, Deandre," said Ken, loudly so everyone heard.

Deandre's parents met everyone. More introductions. More thank-yous. Small talk about the drive up from Petersburg. Kelly stood quietly, not looking at the cooker.

Finally, Kelly went over to Big Tom. She spoke to him softly through the open window, his face buried in a white handkerchief. "We have to get started, honey," she said tenderly. "We have to say goodbye. It's time."

Big Tom nodded. He stuffed the damp handkerchief in his inside jacket pocket, gathered up his crutches, and opened the door. With red, puffy downcast eyes, he crutched over to group. Kelly walked beside him, grave and silent. Bev, Myrna, and Deandre had never seen Big Tom like that. They'd always seen him walking, slowly and thoughtfully, but walking. Mostly in shorts, with his prosthetic in full view. But walking upright, always walking. Never had they seen him on crutches with his pants leg pinned up.

Slowly, carefully, Big Tom went straight to Deandre and hugged him, crutches and all. "Thank you for looking after my baby," he croaked. "You're welcome," Deandre said, his voice breaking, then he helped Big Tom into the seat next to Kelly. Everyone else sat down. Deandre went to the cooker and faced the group. "This is a messed-up day," he began. "Kelly, Big Tom, I am so sorry we are here."

Kelly and Big Tom nodded.

"When I saw the flag on the wall in the pavilion," continued Deandre, "I knew it would help. It would be something good you can remember Baby Rose by. I'm going to fold it for you, Kelly, like they do in the Army. I know how to do it. Dad showed me how."

Heads nodded. Deandre's father straightened in his chair, a proud dad watching his son. All eyes were on Deandre as he folded the flag into a child-sized triangle of white stars on a blue field and handed it to Kelly. "This is from us to you," he said.

"Thank you, D, for thinking of this," said Kelly, her voice quavering. "We will treasure it always," she said, clutching the flag in her lap.

Tearing up, Deandre went to the empty seat between his parents, the sergeant major and the detective, getting a proud squeeze on each leg from both of them.

Reverend Carr went to the cooker and delivered his eulogy and blessing. With the practice of a kind-hearted man who had counseled grieving families for decades, Reverend Carr spoke about Big Tom and Kelly, the strength of their faith, their trust in God's will, and the comfort they could receive knowing that Baby Rose was with Jesus in heaven.

Then it was Ken's turn.

A bitter wind gusted like a series of sighs over the land. In the distance the browns and grays, blacks and greens of a wintry forest gave way to the bluish haze for which those Virginia mountains were named. A bright, burning sun hung high in the cloudless sky.

Standing next to the cooker at the center of the funeral amphitheater that he had created for Big Burn Funeral Services, Ken Keeney looked out over the rolling vista of his beloved farm, the cherished land his people had settled, and gathered before him, the sad faces of friends and family he loved best. "We know why we're here," he said, sonorously, "but we don't know why we're here."

"We're here because of grief," he continued on, a tad too loudly, as though nervous about getting it right. "And we know a lot about grief," he added. "Because we see a lot of it. Like almost every day. Really what we do here is we manage grief. And we're good at it. And the grief we manage is because people die. And that means death is here... like almost every day. Heck, we have death waiting for us right now in the walk-in. We got a funeral to do tomorrow, right, Deandre?"

Deandre nodded as Kelly and Big Tom, sitting side by side, had the same simultaneous puzzled expression. Ray and Bonnie shared a sideways glance. The rest wrinkled their foreheads. Pastor Carr's jaw dropped at the mention of death in the walk-in.

"Daddy," interrupted Kim, "not so much about the business."

"Right, right," said Ken, with a sheepish shrug, "I know, Kimmy. I know. I'm sorry. I just get too focused sometimes. Okay, let me start over. We know why we're here, but we don't know why we're here," he said, again quite formally.

Kim motioned her head toward Big Tom and Kelly. Ken nodded at her hint. "But today it's not about business," he continued. "It's about Tom and Kelly and Baby Rose. So, really, it's about us, too."

Big Tom, holding hands with Kelly, reached back with his free hand and had a good long scratch at the back of his head. Kelly shifted in her seat. Ken gestured clumsily toward the cooker. "And while we know what we're about to do, we don't know why we have to do it," he said.

Kim, lips pressed tightly together, gave him a cautionary head shake.

"We are sad beyond words because we lost something we loved very much," said Ken. "We lost Baby Rose. Even though we never met her, we all loved her very much."

Heads began to nod in tentative agreement.

"We're here today, Kelly and Tom, for you," said Ken somewhat theatrically. Then he threw up his hands and said, "Heck, I can't do this like some big thing. Not today, not with you. This is us."

He went directly to Big Tom and put his hand on his shoulder, and speaking as though they were sharing a sun tea quencher on the tailgate of his truck he said quietly and calmly, "We know how much you loved Baby Rose. We saw your happiness when you were getting ready for her."

Kelly and Big Tom looked up at Ken, their boss, their benefactor, the most generous man they knew, with trust in their eyes.

"And we were happy for you," he continued. "Because she was in your life, we saw how happy you were. We shared in your happiness. Without even meeting her, Baby Rose made us all so happy. And now she's gone and we don't know why.

"Kelly and Tom, thank God you are strong in your faith. Reverend Carr, thanks for coming here and strengthening their faith in this painful time. I wish I was as good at strengthening folks in their faith as you are, but, heck, I'm just a Christmas tree farmer with a really good side business."

"Daddy," cautioned Kim.

"Yes, honey, you're right," said Ken. "Sorry. But the business is part of this. This land is our place. Our home. Our farm. Our worksite. It feeds our families. It feeds our love for each other. And it will be Baby Rose's resting place. We can spread her ashes here and she will be part of this farm, this beautiful land... that we all love till we are all together again in heaven."

Heads nodded.

"At this, Ken paused for a moment and added, "Basically that's forever as far as I'm concerned."

Kelly reached over and held Big Tom's hand.

"And don't worry about me selling the farm," Ken said quickly. "No matter how big an offer I get, and I do get offers, and some are big offers, I'll never sell."

"Daddy," pleaded Kim, as the puzzled looks returned to almost every face.

"But here's what I really want to say," continued Ken, "whatever you need from me, you got it. Kelly, if you and Tom want some time off to go down to Texas to be with your folks, I'll pay for your tickets. And you can take as much time as you need. We can slow things down with the expansion. This has been a lot to take in."

Kelly and Tom nodded, relief on their faces.

"But let me just tell you this, and I say it as someone who lost loved ones. More than once." At that, Ken paused and drew a deep breath while Kim and Bonnie laser focused on his words.

"I made a huge mistake when Karen died," he said, his voice going soft. "And that is, I surrendered my joy. I got scared because I'd lost so much. And that was a big thing with me and Aurie, and it spilled over and hurt Bonnie. For a long time I denied myself joy. And that hurt my children — both of them. I was selfish. I paid more attention to my grief and fear than to my joy, than to our joy. And I let that separate me from people who loved me, who needed me. And it was a huge mistake.

"Basically, I took the easy way. And understand this, no one and nothing can take your joy from you. You do that to yourself. You surrender it, or you don't surrender it. So, Tom, Kelly, don't do it. Don't do what I did. Be strong. You will have babies. You will be wonderful parents. You will. You will have joy again. We will help you."

Heads nodded in unison.

"Kelly and Tom, you're going to get through this. We're a family that's a business and a business that's a family. We love you and we are here for you. And now, I hate to do this, but I have to: It's time to say goodbye to your little one, to our little one. D, go ahead."

Kelly and Big Tom froze in their seats. Stoically Deandre got up from his chair and went to the front end of the cooker.

"Wait," cried Kelly. And, still clutching the folded flag, she jumped up and ran to Baby Rose's tiny, shrouded body. "Goodbye," she said, kissing her fingertips and brushing them on Rose's shroud. "Goodbye, Rose. Mama loves you." And then pulling a single yellow rose from one of the bouquets, she returned to her seat.

Deandre crouched under the cooker and lit the pyre. Fanned by the wind and the accelerants, the flames leaped greedily up through the iron grate. Smoke, black and ominous, burst through the carpet of roses. Within moments, they had wilted, burned, and disappeared. The inferno surged higher, fueled by the woodpile below. Blue flames erupted around the tiny, shrouded corpse. The wind gusted mightily, and then in a burst of phosphorescent brilliance, Baby Rose vanished, right before their eyes. Burned into nothingness. One moment she was there, the next, gone, as though she had never really been there at all.

Disbelieving eyes followed the billowing smoke upwards. Where was she? But the answer was not in the smoke, not on the red hot iron grill. There was no answer. There was only fire, a huge roaring, all-consuming fire. It was the most awful sight any of them had ever beheld, and yet it was beautiful beyond compare. The beauty was in what they witnessed.

And what they felt.

A calm settled over that gathering, a tranquility like they had never known. It was their acceptance of death. The iron fist squeezing Big Tom's heart had vaporized as his tiny baby's body disappeared in front of his eyes. The worst was done. She was gone. He had to accept it.

He had no choice.

No one ever does.

Big Tom, Kelly, Ray, Bonnie, and everyone else sat silent and immobile before that pyre. No one spoke. No one moved. They remained rigid as stone, watching the flames, watching the wind-beaten, black smoke spiraling crookedly into the blue sky. For a teeny, tiny baby, it was a big burn.

Thirty-Three

"He doesn't look right without his antlers," said Bonnie.

"Kind of stripped bare," agreed Ray.

"Like a doe," said Bonnie.

"Yeah, but we won't forget Old Methuselah," said Ken. "I got his antlers, sawed them off, and I'll hang them on the barn."

"Spirit animal," said Ray as he lit the pyre under the deer carcass.

"Yeah, I saw him laying out there, I just couldn't leave him for critter food," said Ken. "It wouldn't have been right."

"No, it wouldn't," agreed Ray.

"Should we say a prayer?" asked Bonnie.

"Sure," answered Ray. "Dear God, please welcome back to deer heaven your beautiful animal Methuselah. We loved him every time we saw him and we will miss him here on Keeney Family Farm. Amen."

"Amen," echoed Bonnie and Ken, then Bonnie added, "Ray, that was a lovely prayer. Only one week since we got married, and you are already better than ever."

"Yes, honey, and I give you all the credit," said Ray, as Ken chuckled in agreement.

The fire roared up around the huge deer. There was no wind on that calm winter day. Smoke enveloped the carcass. Flames blackened the fur. "I'll spread his ashes in the Memory Garden," said Ray.

"Good idea," agreed Ken. "He made a lot of babies in there."

"Circle of life," agreed Ray.

"Speaking of babies," asked Ken, "Did you find a place you like?"

"Yes," said Bonnie. "Way up at the top of the meadow by the pine grove. And, Daddy, that was a lovely wedding present. Thank you."

"You're welcome," said Ken. "Happy to do it. I thought you guys would wind up there. That was Wells land at one point."

Ray nodded. "I knew," he said. "Didn't know you knew."

"Yeah, I knew," said Ken. "Our family knew the history. When Big Tom came back from Iraq and started working here, well, I kind of thought it would be him who would eventually get it, but here you are, my son-in-law. You get it."

"Ray is going to build us a big house up there," said Bonnie, "and I'm going to fill it with babies. Lots and lots of babies."

"Is that right? You want a big family, Ray?" asked Ken.

"Heck yeah, Ken," said Ray. "We're going to live up there where we can look at those beautiful mountains. All we got to do is burn up a bunch of dead people, make a bunch of money, raise a houseful of outrageous kids, send them down your way every chance we get so I can squeeze in some hunting and fishing, and everything will be hunky dory. Best of all, I get to do it all with Mrs. Bonnie Wells by my side."

Ken and Bonnie smiled broadly. "That was a fun wedding," said Ken.

"Crazy and quick, just like us," agreed Bonnie. "Vegas is known for that."

"Yes, it is," agreed Ken. "Okay, I got to get running to pick up Kim at the airport," he said. "Sounds like she's going to need some cheering up after ending it with Anthony."

"Oh, shoot," said Bonnie. "I was hoping that would work out better."

"Yeah, he wanted her to stay down there with him," said Ken. "And once she got a look around, she knew it wasn't her place. She gave him the 'let's be friends' line."

"We'll, it is Tasmania," said Bonnie.

"That was most of it," agreed Ken. "I think she likes being around here a lot more than she realized. Let's give her a thoughtful welcome back home."

"We will," said Bonnie. "We will. I'll bring her along with me and Kelly for some girl stuff. I'm on cheer-up duty these days."

"That's a good idea," Ken said over his shoulder, then he climbed in his truck and drove off with a honk.

"Oh, shoot for Kim," said Bonnie.

"Tasmania," said Ray. "That was never going to work out."

"No, I guess not," said Bonnie. "It's just she was so excited."

"Kim Keeney will be fine," said Ray.

"Yes, she will," said Bonnie. "So will Kelly. And I got to start talking to them about our church wedding this summer."

"We're definitely doing that, another one?"

"Yes, Ray," said Bonnie, "in our church with Reverend Carr."

"I liked that Elvis guy at the chapel."

"Yes, Danny was perfect for us, and Daddy was a good sport about everything. But this will be in church, and to do that, you have to be baptized. Are you baptized?"

"What do you mean?"

"Baptized, Ray, in the name of Jesus. You know with the water on your head."

"I don't know," said Ray, with a thoughtful pull at his chin. "I don't think so. I'd be surprised if Jimmy and Lori pulled that off."

"Yeah, I don't know if I am either," sighed Bonnie. "Reverend Carr won't marry us in church until we are."

"Can't we just do it ourselves?"

"Uh, I'm pretty sure we can't. Baptism has to be done the church way, Ray."

Ray laughed. "Okay, I'll call Reverend Carr. What are we doing now?"

"I don't know, but I am not skinny dipping in this weather. This is cold for a Vegas girl."

"You know, I got a wooden tipi over there. I'm part Indian. And I got a fur pile in there that gets real hot real fast."

"Oh yeah?"

"Yeah."

Thirty-Four

"That water is just about but not quite freezing," said Ray, as he closed the door to his yurt.

"I can't believe we are doing this," said Bonnie, who was seated on top of the fur pile on Ray's bed. "When you told me my Valentine's Day gift was to get baptized together, I didn't think it would be in the farm pond."

"Surprise! Happy Valentine's Day!" Ray said with a grin.

"Are they ready for us?"

"Reverend Carr is standing there, waiting," said Ray. "We just got to run out on the dock and jump in. Kelly has got our bath robes. We put them on. He says a couple prayers. Boom, it will be the fastest baptism he's ever done."

"I don't know how you talked me into this polar bear swim thing," said Bonnie. "I'm never doing this again."

"Well, it's our baptism," said Ray. "We'll only do it once."

"And everybody is there, D's parents too?"

Ray nodded. "Right there with D."

"I'm so glad they made it," said Bonnie, shivering.

"Well, I think it's more their chance to say goodbye before those guys leave for Big Burn Florida," said Ray. "Partly they came to see us get baptized. But mostly they want to see D off."

"Big Burn Ocala," corrected Bonnie.

"Is that what we're calling it?"

"Yeah, that's what Kim decided on," said Bonnie. "She wants to name them after the nearest city. She says that's how you start a business empire."

"Well, she's going to be CEO and we get the farm," said Ray.

"I got a little more out of Daddy than that."

"You did?"

"Honey, I was born and raised in Vegas. First thing I learned is the house always wins. Guess what, we're the house."

Ray stuck his head out the door of the yurt for a look-see. Friends and family bundled against the cold were clustered around the swim dock.

"Hurry up," yelled Big Tom. "It's cold out here. We're waiting."

"We're coming," yelled Ray. "She's bashful."

"She's not bashful," Big Tom yelled back, with half the crowd, including Kim, Ken, Deandre, Bev, Myrna, and Kelly catcalling at the suggestion Bonnie was bashful. The rest just laughed.

"They're not buying that you're bashful," said Ray.

In answer, Bonnie stood up and unbuttoned her dress. Ray took off his clothes. But when Bonnie was about to slip into her bathing suit Ray saw a spider web of blue veins on her breasts. "Hey, what's going on with your boobies," he said in alarm.

Bonnie looked down and smiled. "Oh, wow," she said, "Look at that. That's me making milk, Ray."

"Milk?"

"Because we're pregnant. It's an early sign when you get veins showing like that."

"You're pregnant!"

"We're pregnant."

The shivering group gathered around the edge of the pond gave a cheer when the door to Ray's yurt was finally flung open. Out walked Ray wearing a white XL T-shirt that hung to his knees. He wore it over a pair of cutoffs. He walked to the edge of the wooden platform that served as his porch and gave the crowd a wave and a smile.

"Come on, Bonnie," yelled Big Tom, who was standing on his prosthetic. Kelly was beside him, leaning into him for warmth. Deandre was there with his parents. He wasn't shivering, not in his Tractor Supply coveralls. Ken and Kim and a couple dozen church friends were watching from behind Reverend Carr.

"Bonnie and Ray, we are ready for you," said Reverend Carr. "Most of all, Jesus is ready for you."

At that, Ray stepped off his porch. "Come on, honey," he called over his shoulder. And with a girlish shriek Mrs. Bonnie Wells charged out of that yurt and jumped on her husband's back for her piggyback run to pond. She wore the same white baptismal XL T-shirt. And like Ray, she wore her bathing suit underneath it.

Beaming, Ray trotted down that path. He had Bonnie bouncing up and down and all over his back, and she was giggling at every step. Ray hit the swim dock, burst into a sprint, and launched them both off the edge into that frigid water.

Gasping and spluttering as they surfaced, Bonnie and Ray Wells, husband and wife, big wet smiles, hair plastered to their heads, looked each other deep in the eyes and let out a simultaneous whoop of pure joy.

THE END

# # #

Author Page

Mike McCormick, a lifelong whitewater kayaker and former national team racer, worked in the White House for for three presidents — George W. Bush, Barack Obama, and Donald Trump — over a span of about 15 years (2002 to 2018.) For his position as a White House Press Office stenographer he had daily West Wing duties and traveled around the world on Air Force One and Air Force Two, including into combat zones. He has written four books about what he witnessed from his unusual vantage point. He is currently recognized by national media as a White House whistleblower of Joe Biden and Barack Obama's criminal activities. He is also the co-founder of Team River Runner, a kayak therapy program for wounded service members at Walter Reed Army Medical Center (2004-2007.) He lives in Washington, D.C.

www.ingramcontent.com/pod-product-compliance
Lightning Source LLC
Chambersburg PA
CBHW051237210726
48290CB00003B/1000